The City Beyond the Gates

N. Roy Clifton

illustrated by Tibor Kovalik

Scholastic-TAB Publications Ltd.
123 Newkirk Road, Richmond Hill, Ontario

Copyright © 1972 by N. Roy Clifton. Third edition, with additions from the play *The City Beyond the Gates* © 1978 by N. Roy Clifton, included by special permission of the author.

Illustrations copyright © 1976 by Scholastic-TAB Publications.

ISBN 0-590-71011-7

Published by Scholastic-TAB Publications Ltd., 123 Newkirk Road, Richmond Hill, Ontario, Canada.

1st printing 1979

Printed in Canada

written for
Jane
on her ninth birthday

Do what you like, says God, but pay the price.
— SPANISH PROVERB.

Cities are sepulchres: They who dwell there be carcasses.
— JOHN DONNE, 1597-8

Contents

Janey-Ann is curious

Janey-Ann was lying on a load of crisp hay, which trembled as the wheels beneath trod the ruts and ridges. The mellow tones of the dinner bell drifted slowly across the field in tiny lumps of sound. The lane was planked across with shadows and roofed by limbs of trees, beneath whose leafy twigs her Uncle Harry ducked his head, as he drove the team. It was the afternoon of her birthday.

"Uncle Harry," she said, looking up at a tuft of cloud melting into the blue, "what are the people like, across the Fence?"

"How should I know, my dear? I have never seen the place, nor those who live there, but through the pales of the Fence, just as you have."

"But you are older, and must have heard stories about them. Why are we different, Uncle Harry?"

"I know one thing," he answered. "From what I can see of their water, and from what I can see of their soil, they don't seem to know how things live, every living thing needing all the others. And look what happens. Our streams are clear: you can see the fish on the bottom, wriggling and glittering in the sun. I've seen one of their streams where here and there it sweeps near the Fence. Their water is grey. It stinks. The only fish you can see are floating on the top, and they're dead. And it often edges up over its banks, and lays down a sheet of mud, smothering everything."

"I have often come here," she said, "for the little narrow field between the trees looks like a road from here to there, though on our side it is overgrown by grass and flowers, and on their side many rains have washed little runnels through it, and it is full of cracks like an old cup. No one has mended it, no one's feet going either way have worn any path for the eye to follow. And they have no nuts or apples — what do they eat? How do they live with no tree-friends, to keep the wind away, to make the air we breathe, and cool us on days like this? And where will the little silver lamps dangle on rainy days?"

"Ah, they're a queer lot, right enough," her uncle said. "I've heard say they're always trying to get the better of their neighbours instead of helping them. They'd skin a louse for its hide and tallow. I've heard say they never sing together, never laugh even."

"Haw there, haw Nell," he cried out to the horses. The waggon lurched out of the lane towards a gate. He pulled the team to a stop, laid the reins on the ladder, put his arm around the girl, and gave her an affectionate pat.

"And what's more," he said, "the place has as many folk as a cat has fleas — and that don't make me think any better of them. You can over-graze any pasture, never mind how good it is. And that's what the place looks like to me — over-grazed pasture."

"Was the Fence to keep them out? Who built it?"

"Nobody built it. It grew. The Fence grew because we think different. There were trees in their country, too, at one time, and no Fence. But the Fence was there in my grandfather's time, and the ground bare, just as it is today. No one I know has crossed over: no one I know would want to."

Down the ladder she climbed, leapt off, and opened the gate. She stood beside it, looking down the long narrow glade that cut through the green and floating woods, to the Fence that barred the way with huge crooked fingers. It was not a Fence made by man, of straight sawn planks nailed in a row, for its pales were like tree trunks, round, ribbed, and gnarled, as if it had not been built at all, but had grown on its own.

From high above on the load, her uncle leaned his head over towards her. "You wouldn't like it over there, would you?"

Her gaze was held by the little field, and the Fence that closed its end. "I'm sure I shouldn't," she began,

" but I wish . . ."

She stopped, astounded. Bare and grey, there was the other country, as clear as if the Fence had sunk out of sight into its roots. But the trees had no leaves, their branches now thrust into the glade at other places, and the soft sigh of the woods had withered away to a snowy silence. She held her breath, to be sure of what she saw, before it vanished.

It was her uncle's voice growing louder that made it fade. "What's wrong? What are you staring at? Why are you all for knowing so much about them folk? You've something up your sleeve, Janey-Ann. What is it now?"

She turned. "Now what could I possibly have up this sleeve?" she said with a smile, waving a bare arm. "But there's something going round my cerebellum. I don't really know what it is. When I find out myself, I'll tell you — perhaps tomorrow."

Her uncle laughed. "Another of your long words," he said. "Are you sure you know what a cerebellum is?"

"It's part of my head. I'm not quite sure what part. Anyway," she said very firmly, "I like the sound of it. I only like long words that sound nice."

He smiled. "Thank you for all your help today, Janey-Ann. Will you take supper with us?"

"Thank you, no," she answered. "There's something I have to do."

After the load had swayed through, she closed the

gate again. Her uncle looked back and waved. "Good-bye," she shouted. He was really her third cousin, four times removed. So they said. But they weren't able to explain clearly what this meant. The grandparents of third cousins were first cousins — that she knew, and that was all. She wondered, now and then, why they had had to remove him four times, but she thought maybe he'd rather not say, so she never asked him. In any case, he made a very nice uncle, and it was an uncle she needed, not a third cousin. So what did it matter?

He slapped the reins on the horses' backs, and she watched the back of the jag of hay, as it plodded away. She walked slowly back to look again into the little field, but the Fence had risen again, blackly obliterating all that lay beyond it.

She finds the Gate

Janey-Ann lay on the grass, where the lace-like leaves above her, bobbing in the restless wind from across the Fence, sprinkled a mat of shifting and winking shadows. A step in front of her nose was the Fence of Unwish.

She saw through the chinks in the Fence a wide unhilled plain, that ran to a straight-ruled horizon. Its grass, where grass there was, was pale, for the rain stayed little while there, and when the sun parched it, the ground was a hard slab, dark-veined by hungry winding slits. It looked as if some giant hand had shorn off the dark, soft, plant-growing cloth which lay on her side of the Fence, and had uncovered a hard yellow table.

Far away, from out the bright yellow plain glowing with sunshine, a tall tower sprang white into the cloudless blue of the sky. "I wonder who lives in the highest room?" she said to herself.

Between her and the tower, she could see waggons,

gliding in some strange way without the horses she was used to seeing in front of them, glittering in the sun, and going so fast you had to turn your head quickly to follow them, and shrinking off into the distance before you had time even to be sure what colour they were. Closer to the Fence were the lips of the ditch where the stream flowed unseen, stealing from it now and then the sickening dungy gas from dried fish. Sometimes she had to close her eyes and hold her breath as a drift of dusty wind from the plain made the little glade around her blurred and gritty.

She felt sorry for the people living beyond the Fence; for she was able to lie down by her stream, and watch the sunlight quivering on the stones at the bottom, drink of the clear water, or touch its coolness to her cheek. She thought of the presents given to her by her brothers and uncles on this her birthday; and she wished she might carry sunseeds, and a tree for them to plant, over to the poor folk who lived where nothing grew.

"But what about the Fence?" thought she. "There's no way to go through it" (and she thrust three of her fingers between two of the pales), "or over it" (and she bent her head back as far as she could, till her eyes rose to the tips of the pales), "or around it" (and she craned her neck either way, and she could see, as Uncle Harry had said, that the Fence had no end). "However," she said to herself, "it will be time enough to see about the Fence, when I have dug the trees, and poured the sunseeds in a bag."

She leapt up and ran back to the cottage (for she never walked whenever it was possible to run). She took a large bag she had woven from reeds (she liked making things, for she had nimble fingers) and filled it with sunseeds. There were sunflower seeds, and grains of wheat, and butternuts, and others too: she called them all sunseeds — they all came from the sun, she said, for it was the sun that ripened them. She dug up a Trembling Aspen Tree. She liked it more than other poplar trees, for the way its round leaves fluttered sideways, which made them twinkle in the sun, and for the smooth pale green bark that gloved its trunk, and for its unceasing gossiping, even in the slightest breeze, when every other tree was still. Other trees grew old, but this always seemed young, like herself. She bundled the earth around the seedling's roots in a wet sack, and put it in a second bag. She threw a few sunseeds to the squirrels, and skipped back to the Fence with a bag in either hand.

"That Fence isn't going to stop me," she said to herself. "The poor people of the stones will be so glad of a tree, and so happy to eat some sunseeds, that I must find a way past the Fence." She dropped the bags to the ground, and set her arms akimbo. "I haven't given it a really good push yet," she thought.

She stood in the middle of where the road had been — the road that no one had used as long as man could remember — pressed both hands flat on the pales, bent one leg, pushed back as hard as ever she could with the other one — and almost fell flat. For they had given way, the pales had given way, and for a waggon length on either side of her, had swung back, like two tall gates, and there was the tall shiny tower, and nothing to stand between it and her any more but a great expanse of pale yellow clay, that now the Fence was open, she reckoned as nothing.

Janey-Ann was not often puffed up, but now she did look rather pleased with herself. "The Gate must have been there all the time. I suppose gates just vanish in fences, if no one uses them or no one wants to use them."

Locked out

She ran back to pick her bags up, and then carried them slowly along the forgotten road, her eyes on the tall tower. A hot wind blew from the land of the tower, that wrapped her bare arms like a warm blanket, blew into her eyes the wisps of her chestnut-coloured hair that were not pulled back in her pony-tail, billowed out the folds of her blue skirt, and tossed the tall heads of grass, that swayed back each time like upside-down pendulums.

Slowly she came to the opening; slowly the Fence rose on either side, and posed a question to her. Her eyes turned from the tower, rose up the tall posts, whose tops thrust up through the sunny upper lofts of the trees. Hung on these posts, like mighty gates, were the two limbs of the Fence that had fallen back. But no posts before had been like these. That was almost an arm that ran along the Gate and held it up, and those two bulges nearly shoulders. Up there, where the leaf-shadows flittered across the creases in the bark like fingers across harp strings, was that a mouth, were those knots or eyes? She couldn't be sure, for every time she looked away and back, the posts never looked the same as they had been. Every time a napkin of light wiped the mouth, it was gone; and when she saw it again, she couldn't be sure whether it was really there or merely remembered. It was almost as if tall straight men, with feet prisoned in the ground, held up the Gates, and gazed each into the eyes of the other.

"I do wish to ride in the shiny waggons, to climb the tall tower, to speak to those who live there, and see if I can help them. I am sure there are some who would want to come back with me. But I'm scared. The Gates might not be there when I come back. I wonder what I should do."

As she was standing there, a sound like the wind rose in a low slow note through the forest. She started, for a voice had spoken, and surely it came from the Gate-Posts, both speaking together from either side of her. The voice was certainly stern, but not unkind: "No gate in the world is ever locked, if she who knocks can pay the porter's price."

"That's odd," she said. "I've never heard before of gate-posts talking; but that's no reason why they shouldn't. Today may be the day that posts begin to talk. Still, if they did say what I thought they said, what do they mean by a price? What have I got that they would want? Now that I think of it, what sort of things would posts need?"

The wind, which had slackened, blew again, a low still whistle through the branches. She turned her head quickly. She was sure she saw a mouth close on one of the Gate-Posts; but the trees clustered thick behind, the breeze jumbled their shadows, and what she saw might have been the quick flight of a bird. And yet the words were clear: "The gates that stand, crave the wish that can move them; the gates that bar, crave the force that can pass them; the gates that live unseen, crave the eye that can find them."

Janey-Ann thought a moment. "That means, I think, that if I wish hard enough to come back, the Gates will open for me. Tell me, Gate-Posts, is that right?"

She waited several minutes, but heard no more voice, only a low soft flute-like note that rose up high, whistled a while, and fell back into silence, as ripples in a pool fall back into flatness.

So she had to make up her own mind. "I think that's what the Gate-Posts meant," she said, and looked at them again. It may have been the shadow thrown by a twig, but she thought she saw a smile on one of the Gate-Posts, just where the mouth would have been. "Thank you, Gate-Post," she said, and walked through.

Now she was in the open, walking not on cool springy grass, nor a harrowed field, that softly absorbed your feet, but a hard yellow rock, often strewn with sharp lumpy pebbles. She trod it with cautious feet. Some-times, beside her feet, in a cleft of the dry clay, tiny stalks of birch or elm, of yarrow or butter-and-eggs, would stretch up to the sun, but never had she seen a flower before on a stem so short and thin. Small still was the tower of white, but along the road that ran the same way as the Fence, the flitting shiny horseless waggons were closer to her, without any slackening to say they had seen her.

Then she thought of the Gate. Was it still open waiting? Her heart suddenly thumped. She was facing back before she knew she had turned. Where was the Gate? There was the Fence, and there were the trees beyond it; but there wasn't any Gate any more. No more than there ever had been.

She dropped her bags and ran back to the Fence. She leant on it, eyes closed, breathing fast and heart beating faster, so hard it ached. Her voice could only whisper, "Gate-Posts, Gate-Posts! Let me back to the duff and the soft clover. This hard floor hates my feet."

There was no answer. She opened her eyes. There were no Gate-Posts to listen to her. Only the wind rose in a low flute-like note, and fell again.

"Maybe I wish too much still to see the people who live among the stones." Her breath and heartbeat were now slower. Her thoughts were slower too, and less fierce. "That must be what they meant," she went on, a little sorry for herself. "I wished more to cross to here, than I really wish now to cross back. My wishes aren't strong enough to spread the Gates, so there's no use coming here again, until they change. Good-bye, Gate-Posts."

Stronger than her sadness for what she had left behind her was excitement, at the thought of the places and people soon to be encountered.

She turned again, and walked slowly toward the city of stone.

A friend appears

It was growing dark, and all the shiny horseless waggons glowed with buttons of yellow light in front, and of red behind. The tower was a pale dream; beyond it the last blue glimmer of day was all that remained of her birthday, and above the tower, in the blue, was a single spark of light from an early planet.

On the peak of the pale tower, like a sudden eye, a white dome lit up; but its mystery was dulled by her weariness. Her feet were covered with dust, and their soles felt raw from walking on the pebbly hardness.

She was at a bridge, where the grey stream flowed under the road. The tree was heavy. Maybe this was a good place to plant it — near the stream where its roots would not parch, and its leaf be green. She left the shoulder of the road, and halfway down the slope of the valley, knelt, dug a hole with her fingers, placed in it some of the dead fish that lay on the grey sand, and pressing its leafy coolness to her cheek with a sigh, rose to her feet, firmed the sand around the stem, and went back to the road.

She had often ridden a waggon on the south road, and watched the floating trees, the jolting of the horses' rumps and flicking of their tails, as the waggon sucked the road into itself. What would she see from one of these fast shiny waggons? It would have been nice to find out; but no one stopped. Could they not see, through the clear walls that closed them in, that she was going the same way as they? In her country waggons would stop, and the teamster would call to wayfarers to climb up the whiffle-tree or ladder on to the rack or load. But he was out in the open air. Perhaps he could see better. Perhaps the man driving horses was going slower and could stop in time, and perhaps it was harder to pass a person by without a word. Here they passed as if she were not there.

All along the road, at some distance from it, and evenly-spaced, was a row of what looked like little houses, not very wide, and only twice as high as she was. She noticed now in front of one, a long flat stone. It looked so much like a bench to sit on, that she left the road, and went over towards it. She put her bags down, and walked curiously around the little house. She found that the side of the house away from the road was not smooth, solid and flat, like the other three, but the whole height and width of the side was covered with a metal grille, like a large coarse screen, through which

16

she could see the darkness inside. Through the grille, from what seemed far away in the centre of the earth, she could hear a steady hum. Too tired for wonder, she went back to the other side, and sat on the stone.

She thought of all the stumps and crooked roots and forks of trees that waited through all the woods for her to sit on. She thought of the lovely birthday party she had had, and of the presents her brothers and uncles had given her that morning, when she came to break-fast. She thought how all this kindness to her had made her wish to help the people of the stones. And here she was, away from home, lost and weary; it was nearly night, and no one cared whether she came or not. Her head sank down to rest on her hands, and her eyes were filled with tears.

She had sat so a long time, and had wept her hanky quite wet, when someone said, "What are you crying for? Is it something I can help you with?"

She looked up. It was a boy. He had green shoes, green shorts, and a green shirt open at the neck. He sat on a seat whose weight was carried by one wheel in front of him, and another behind him. He later called this machine a Galopede. But his eyes! A square smooth screen covered each eye, like a window. It made him seem far away, unknowable, as if he were closed off from the world outside where she was. And yet, as she looked more intently, she could see that his eyes, like hers, were green-grey.

"I came to see the people of the tall house," she said, her tears brought to a stand by having to find words. "It is still very far away, and my feet are sore. I am tired and hungry, and it's growing dark and cold, and no one will give me a ride, and I have nowhere to stay, and there isn't a Gate in the Fence any more, so I can't go home."

"Do you come from the Tree-Land across the Fence?" His voice was eager.

"Yes."

"I often go there to look at the trees. I sometimes sleep where the branches hang thickly over the Fence. But where is the Gate?"

"It was there when I wished the Fence to let me through; but I couldn't wish hard enough to make it let me back."

The boy shook his head. "I've wished hard enough to go to where the trees are, but I never saw any gate."

"That's because there are other things you wish more." It made her more cheerful to be able to tell him something she knew and he didn't. "I know — the Gate-Posts told me. That's why I can't go back. I wish too much to see the tall house."

"I wonder," he said, "if I could go through the Fence without seeing the Gate, if you showed me where it was."

"When I turned and saw the Gate was gone," she answered, "I ran back and I pushed and pushed, right where the Gate had been, and the Fence was as strong as ever. I think the Gate is there for those who can see it, and not there for those who can't."

"Do you mean," he said, "that a Gate could be there and not be there, at the same time?"

"Yes, I think so."

The Green Boy sat on the ground facing her. He picked up the empty bag and said, "What a nice bag! I have never seen one like it. What is it made of?"

"It is made of reeds. I wove it myself."

"But it's empty. I know: it's to take things back in."

"No," she replied. "I brought a tree in it, but it's planted."

"Poor thing. It's going to be lonely here. Where did you plant it?"

"Oh, it's a long way back — by the stream."

"What was it like?" he asked.

"Quite small — only this high."

"You must take me to see it," said the Green Boy, smiling and rising to his feet. "But come with me now and have something to eat. And you watch that Galopede as you sit down on it. I can see it, and I can feel it as I sit on it. But you may be sitting on nothing."

"Well, you be ready to catch me, just in case," she said, much more cheerful now.

He showed her how to sit behind him, and hold on to a padded ring in front of her. As the Galopede sped along through the dimming light, she felt the quivering air stroking her legs and her face, which was moist from tears. It was like a long long cat, she thought, rubbing its fur against her.

And at last she was having her ride, not in one of the closed-in waggons, but on something much nicer. It had its yellow eye in front, and a red one behind, but you could see all around you and above you. But what she saw was a little disappointing; on either side, the rows of little houses, all the same size and colour, the flat land with nothing growing to catch the eye in all the yellow waste, and the smooth road without even a bump. Then she looked up, and she saw a softly-glowing white cloud floating along without sound or hurry at the same pace as she and the boy were travelling. "At least that's the same as at home," she thought, "and it's really nicer than anything else here."

From the cloud her eye came back to the half moon of the white shining dome on the tower ahead, that seemed, as they rode, as if rising higher all the time in the night sky.

How it came about

Janey-Ann felt better after she had washed her feet in hot water and filled her stomach. Out of a white box in the wall, the Green Boy's father took some white porridge-like stuff to put on her plate.

"This," he said, "is Mish-Mash. It will fill you up, so you won't be hungry."

He then placed a large white ball on the table. It rolled over quickly, suddenly stopped, and opened up of itself. Inside were five hollows, each holding a different-coloured powder. "The grey one," he said, "is to pass what you eat through your bowels. It won't go through otherwise. The others are vitamins, protein, and minerals, and the bright red one is Flavrex, which makes your mouth water, and wets your food. Without it, you wouldn't want to eat the rest at all, and our chemists tell us it's the perfect flavour."

"Could I try a bite without the red?" she asked.

"You're quite right," she said, after tasting them all.

"Every one of them tastes like — sawdust. Well, the way sawdust looks, for I've never really tasted any. But now I must, the next time I see some, or perhaps the next time I saw some."

She smiled, but they didn't smile with her. She didn't say, for it might hurt their feelings, that the red powder was well enough, but it lacked the joy of a juicy black cherry or summer apple, warm from the tree.

This all set her wondering. Where did the powders grow? And why wouldn't their bowels work? — she never thought about hers. She was told the powders came from rocks, but the other question came to her when her mouth was full, and when it was empty again, she was on to something else, and forgot to ask it.

"Before I can answer all your questions," the boy's father said after supper, "and before you ask more, I'll have to go back a little way, and perhaps, when I have finished, some of your questions may have answered themselves. Fair-Look used to be called the City of the Giant, because all around us is a Giant. He cannot be seen, but he is in the air, and in the earth, perhaps even in us, and he is stronger than we are."

"How do you know?" she said.

"Well, things happen that are much beyond our power to make happen, and sometimes against our wishes. Some power outside ourselves must have made them happen. And we have found that by certain charms or magic, we can — as we say — awaken and command the Giant, so that things happen as we wish them to."

"What do you mean by charms or magic?" Janey-Ann asked him.

"I don't know much about it — it is taught only to those who are trained as Kemaths, or priests. But I once saw one of the charms they write when wakening the Giant — it was all letters and figures of different sizes with dashes and crosses between them. And I have heard that in their secret rooms, they make use of water, air, fire, and rock, and forces that can't be seen.

"At first we were glad, for the Giant gave so much. He taught us how to dig black lumps from the earth to warm us and cook our food. We offered the Giant rocks, trees, and much black soil, and he turned them to machines that made us clothing, waggons, furniture and houses. We stopped planting or harvesting crops, when he taught us how to make our food from the black lumps, and he gave us black water to drive our machines and waggons, instead of using our muscles. "

"So," said Janey-Ann, "you never grow tired any more?"

The Green Boy answered quickly, "Oh yes we do, but not in the same way."

"Ambion is right," his father continued. "As time passed, we came to see that for everything the Giant gave us, he took something from us. We worked, not in the warm sun, but in the cold glare of huge rooms underground. Instead of air cleansed by the trees and rain, we breathed the sacred fumes from the trees and lumps burnt as the Giant commanded, and our lungs were blackened. And each year he exacts the life of one person in every fifty of us. Each of us thought the one to die would not be he, so carried away were we by all the Giant had given us; but each day some of us — and none of us knows which will be chosen — are thrown to the middle of the road, and a gallop-waggon runs over and crushes them. This we call the tax.

"And yet, as Ambion says, even with less work and more things, we still were tired, tired sometimes even of living. We were afraid, restless, untrusting of one another; we didn't seem at home in this place — the Giant had stolen our happiness, and we hadn't known it.

"To cure this, he made us Forgetters of many kinds — "

The Green Boy interrupted his father: "I'll show you some of these, Janey-Ann. Where I work there are big screens on which we see people moving round and hear them talking; and as we listen and watch, we come to believe that our lives are like those we see on the screen, and it is hard, sometimes, to look around us and see that they are not."

His father smiled and went on. "I must shorten my story. We came to be sick now of new diseases. We besought the Giant, and he cured us, by placing us inside huge machines, or by giving us certain fungi to swallow. These are so small that seven hundred and seventy-seven will just barely be seen on the point of a needle, and they raise them on strawberry-flavour jelly which, the Kemaths tell us, is all they will eat."

Janey-Ann thought from this that strawberries at least must be grown in Fair-Look, but the boy said no.

"Then how do you know the jelly is strawberry-flavoured?"

"Well, when we buy it, that is what it says on the label," he said, "but whether it is really what a strawberry tastes like, I don't know. How does a strawberry taste?"

"Let us finish one thing at a time," said his father. "Whether by machine or fungi, the Giant would only save nine in every ten of us. This was the new tax: the tenth person, before he is twenty, cries aloud in pain, lives in pain for many months, and then dies. He turns black, and by the Giant's command, is laid underground in the empty galleries from which we have dug the Giant's black lumps.

"When first we sought the Giant's help, who was to know that this was where it would bring us? And now these horrible things happen so often, that we think no more of them than we do of a shower of rain. But few of us are happy people."

Janey-Ann asked him, "Each time the priests asked you to do something new, couldn't you have told them you didn't wish to change and be frightened all the time .

— as you are now?"

"Who was to know," the boy's father said, "that when one change was made others would happen too at the same time? The Kemaths, I do not doubt, thought that what they did would make our lives better. They said nothing about the tax; perhaps they didn't know about it themselves. And we always hoped that what was new would be better, and in some ways it was. New things are never better or worse than the old: they are better and worse. Perhaps at some point we should have told them, 'This is enough: we didn't intend all this.' But we often desire new things more, because they are new."

"Yes," was all Janey-Ann could say, for she thought of herself and the Gate. "But why," she cried, "must you stay in this horrible place, when you know it is horrible. Come and live with us in the Tree-Land."

The father's mouth smiled, but not his eyes. "You are a kind girl to ask me, but all my friends are here; we live all under the same fear: if I leave here, I live without friends."

"You can make new friends — and maybe better ones."

She wasn't sure if he heard her, for he went on as if she hadn't spoken: "And I am less well than I was and older. I couldn't go back to the work we did before the Giant woke and worked for us. I may as well die one way as another."

"Yes," said Janey-Ann. "My mother and father are

dead. I know we must all die. We cannot choose there. But we can choose the way in which we live, and the way we die. You are living . . . "

She was interrupted by a whistle-like sound that loudened into a shriek, which all but wiped from the air a whip-like snap, a thud, and a cry of pain, that came at the highest pitch of the sound. Then it died away.

"Ambion," said the boy's father, very sharply for one so gentle, "you should have shut the door. It is the tax," he said to Janey-Ann. "It is better not to hear it."

The Laws

Janey-Ann looked at the boy. He rose and closed the door. "Don't worry, Janey-Ann," he said. "They cannot tax you, only us."

He looked at his father. "I think she is right, father. And now I am sure you do too. How can you feel this way and stay here?"

His father said nothing. Janey-Ann could feel pain in the silence. She spoke, she could not say whether more to relieve him or herself: "Why do you all wear little square windows over your eyes?"

He gave her a smile, as if he felt what had led her to speak. She noticed his eyes, nesting in deep shadows, his grey hair, the yellow-grey of his face (not ruddy-brown like her Uncle Harry's), and the deep hard lines around his eyes and mouth, gentled only when he smiled. "Though I suppose," she said to herself, "it's what a face looks like nearly all the time, which tells you what a person is really like."

"It is one of the Kemarch's laws. The windows, we were told, were to guard our eyes from the sun, and we did find that our eyes were sore in the sun. That was true, and that is why our houses are under the ground. But I think there was another reason. Before the law was passed, I used to see things I never see now, now that I'm wearing windows."

. "What things?" said Janey-Ann curiously.

"Well, the Kemarch's laws were enforced by the Golden Men I spoke of. Since the law for guarding the citizens' eyes was passed, I have never seen another Golden Man. Yet all the laws they made us obey, we are still being made to obey. Surely the Golden Men were in the street a moment ago."

"Have you ever seen a Golden Man?" she asked the boy.

"No," he said. "I have always worn windows."

She turned back to the father. "Is there more about the Giant?"

He didn't answer at once, as if he didn't wish to tell what was to come. "After a time," he said slowly, "it looked as though we should soon come to an end of our trees, of the black earth, and the black water from under the earth. We sent envoys to other cities to buy from them. They said either they had no more than they needed for themselves, or else demanded in return more than we could pay.

"Then the Giant showed us how to stand in line and

make weapons. With them we killed or subdued men of other cities, and took from them what we needed."

"That was wicked," said Janey-Ann, "wicked of you to do it, and of the Giant to help you."

"Do not blame the Giant. The killing is not his, it is ours. Long before we woke him up, we fought and killed. The Giant only helps us do it faster and kill more. He has not made us worse or less wise, but only more baneful to one another."

"But why should you need to kill anyone?" Janey-Ann cried. "In my country, I am welcome to eat at any house along the road. Is not that what the seeds and roots are for? And when food is short — for frost, rain or wind may spoil the harvest — it wouldn't be right for me to eat more than my neighbours. If I did, I'd feel they'd never want to speak to me any more, or work or dance with me. How could I ever eat again at their table? It would build a fence between them and me like that between you and us."

"When we go from home," the father gently said, "we take a bag of flattened rocks with us, and these will buy the food we need. Some people do nothing else but keep food ready for travellers."

"Well, it's much easier to carry nothing," said Janey-Ann, more and more convinced that the Tree-Land was better in every way. It was her first visit to another country, and that is the time when our own ways always seem better to us than anyone else's: we may be less certain later on. She weighed the matter for a while, and there were three silences, each one different. Then she spoke.

"I suppose, if you are going to win your fights, the Giant makes you pay another Tax."

"Yes."

"I'm sure it's something nasty, so I don't want you to tell me what it is," she answered, and after a pause, "I suppose he's the kind of Giant you want."

"There may be a Giant in your land also," the father said, "who may be asleep and cannot hear you."

"Or do you suppose," she thought to herself, "that like your Golden Men, the Giant is there and awake, but cannot be seen, and still may be giving us all we need? Anyway," she ended aloud, "if we had a Giant, I can think of nicer things to ask for."

The Stranger

At home, the low red sun shining through her window woke her up. Now she woke in a dark room; she knew from what she could feel that it was not her own bed; she was frightened. She cried out but no one came. Yesterday then unreeled itself in her memory. It came back that here they made their own day and night. She pushed a knob near her bed, and light came on.

She was longer than usual putting her clothes on, for all the Green Boy and his father had said kept coming back. She opened the door, and remembered that underground you have to climb up to go out. She called Ambion's name without reply, went up, and found food set out in the kitchen. Beside it was a note: "For Janey-Ann. Father and I have to go to work. Don't go away before we come home." On top of the note he had left a dried and pressed oak leaf.

She took a spoonful of Mish-Mash, but it only reminded her that if she ever reached home again, she must be sure to try some sawdust. After a single mouthful, she gave up and ate some sunseeds. She was now more curious than ever to see the City of the Giant. She left a note for the Green Boy, and went out.

The road soon went underground, and now she heard music. She was unable to tell where it was from. She thought she would listen till the end of the piece, but it kept going on, with very little change, a quiet easy sort of music that, when she closed her eyes, made her think of floating away with pale grey curtains all round her. So she decided to stop listening, open her eyes, and go on, which was just as well, for she found it played in the streets all day.

Only women shared the street with her, and they were few. "They are odd-looking," she said to herself. "All bright and prettied up like new dolls."

One of the women passed. Janey-Ann turned and kept looking at her back. "You see," she told herself. "They pass you by without looking at you. I don't think there's anyone there to look. She was like a face borrowed from someone else, a face without a person. I wonder if she knows she isn't there." This time she laughed aloud.

There was someone there though, for at this moment the woman turned, and gave Janey-Ann a glare, as if she had known someone was looking at her. "Quite right," said Janey-Ann, as she turned quickly round and went on. "I know I shouldn't stare at people. It makes them feel queer, and that isn't nice. And anyway, I'm the one that should feel queer here, for I'm the one that's different."

The street was wide and coloured red. At each side of it was a white walk for people. Lining the streets now were buildings of white stone, with hard stone-like fronts you could see through.

In the first front she came to, there was food. On pale yellow packages were the bright red words, *MISH-MASH*. "The food of a hundred flavours" was written underneath in small letters. "What a fib," she said to herself. "How can they say such a thing, when anyone who tastes it knows it hasn't any flavour?"

Where two roads crossed at right angles, a square opening in the roof let in the sky and the sun, and the tall tower was now so near that she could see it through the opening, shining against the blue. At each corner of the cross-roads, running a little down each street, was an angle of wall as high as her chest, and on top of the walls flower-boxes. She ran towards the flowers as soon as she saw them, and bent the nearest one towards her to smell. It came away in her hand. It had no smell. It wasn't alive at all, but an imitation, made of some tough pliable coloured material. She turned away to one of the fronts.

It was now that she met the Stranger. She was puzzling over something they said you could either breathe or chew or drink, when a movement in the corner of her eye made her turn. A tall man stood beside her, legs apart, and hands behind his back. He wore only a white cloth around his middle. His skin was dark brown as of one much in the sun. A stern man, she thought: his lips were straight but not thin; slowly his eyes locked on hers, and she felt their force like a strong but pleasant wind.

"You are a stranger," he said quietly.

"Yes, and so are you, for you aren't wearing any windows, and you aren't dressed like the others. Indeed," she said with a little giggle, "you almost aren't dressed at all."

He laughed. "If it is strange not to think or act or dress like most other people, I suppose I am a stranger of sorts," he said, "and yet I was born here." He looked quickly up and down the street. She followed his glance, but the street was empty now, even of women.

"Are you looking for someone?" she enquired politely.

His eye was still searching into the distance, but a smile hovered now on one side of his mouth, and he said, "Not in the sense that I want to find him. It's more that someone's looking for me — and I hope in the wrong place. It must be hard for him, never quite sure where to find me. Not, of course, that I want him to."

"Then he isn't a friend of yours?"

"No, not a friend; just a man from the Stationary

Office. They're always trying to stop me changing things."

"I know what it is," she said. "You're not wearing your windows, and the Golden Men are after you."

"Well, that'll do for a start," said the Stranger, looking at her in surprise. "How very well informed you are for one so recently arrived."

"Oh, I know all about this place," Janey-Ann replied, half serious, half in jest. "I don't think I like it very well, but it's not very hard to understand."

"However," he went on, "that's not the only thing I do that upsets the Kemarch."

"Who is he?"

"He is head of this place, the Chief Servant of the Giant."

"I hadn't heard of him yet," she said, "but why is he looking for you?"

"Well, I have no wish-marks, you see." He touched the back of his neck — she wondered why. "I use nothing the Kemarch makes, so he cannot force me to work in his making-places. I go where I will, and I cannot be caught unless I choose to be. And when I talk to people, many of them too decide not to use the Kemarch's things. Now you'd think this would be less work for him; you'd think he'd thank me for it."

"And he doesn't?" She matched his mood with mock sympathy.

He looked up to the peak of the tower, smiled, and

shook his head. "Bless you, no. He doesn't like it at all. You know, because you come from the trees, that it's when a bee has ceased to buzz noisily around and sits quietly on a flower, that he is gathering nectar, which is what he is here for. But this the Kemarch doesn't seem to know — I wonder if he has ever seen a bee. He can't abide people who don't look busy and sound busy. As soon as he gives them one silly thing, he gets them running after another one. Only thus can he keep them all working. If he were running a bee-hive, he'd have the bees digging holes in the ground, flying to the moon, diving to the bottom of the sea, and filling their honey-sacs with everything else in the world except honey."

"It sounds very complicating," said Janey-Ann.

"Oh, it is. It really doesn't have to be, you know, but he's very good at making simple things hard to understand. He could write a book about eating, and after you'd read it, you'd never be able to eat again, he'd make it sound so hard." And he laughed softly.

"You know, you're the first person I've heard laugh in this place," she told him. "But the Kemarch, you said, is the servant of the Giant? Is the Kemarch really doing what the Giant wants?"

"I say no," he answered. "I too am a servant of the Giant. I am one of the few who really respect the Giant, of whom few people here ever even think. They take what the power brings them without caring where it comes from. But surely a Giant who can do such things as they can see around them — it is true they cannot see the intricate beauty of a tree, but there are clouds above them, they know the irresistible power of their machines — these are things to be thought about, marvelled at, eagerly sought, out of their greatness and wonder, beside which we are puny. When I hear the whisper of leaves, or see the rosy lightning darting low in the sky, or smell the scented mould where seeds grow, I seem to feel the Giant close to me, and sometimes I seem to vanish myself, and instead of me thinking of the Giant, there is only the Giant, only One, of which I am part, like the leaf or twig of a tree."

He paused, lost in thought, as if he had forgotten she was there, then caught her eye, shook his head and went on. "To choose the Kemarch's junk instead of this, and risk their lives for it — oh it's — it's like walking all day for a drink of dirty water because you cannot see the clear bubbling well in your own garden."

He laughed again. "I mustn't let them upset me. I don't mind the Kemarch half as much as his people. He's the best man of them all. He knows quite well, for he's a clever man, all he has had to give up, so he could reach the room under the dome. He thinks (just as I do) that he's made the better choice; and no one can change him. And if these poor deprived and imprisoned people must have the things that destroy them, he is as honest a man as any to give them what they ask for. But as for me, I shall still choose my own way and speak what I know, and his will shall not replace mine."

"I don't understand all that," said Janey-Ann. "Let's start right at the beginning again. What are wish-marks?"

At that moment, men in golden-coloured suits appeared in all four streets, and began running towards them. The Stranger had seen them too. He turned and smiled at her as before, and spoke his last words without haste.

"That, I'm afraid, you'll have to find out for yourself," he said, "for I have to go. I see company coming. I have no taste for crowds, and I don't like the way this crowd's dressed." He nodded solemnly. "The Kemarch's doing better today. It took him quite a while, but he did find me. I'll give him nine out of ten — it'll encourage him. I can't give him ten, for I don't think he's going to catch me — not this time."

Then he grinned. Before she could open her mouth to say good-bye, he was up on one of the little walls, had leapt from there to grasp the edge of the roof, had pulled himself up, and was gone.

The wish printer

As the steps grew louder, Janey-Ann shrank back to the corner of the two streets, feeling as if the Golden Men approaching from four directions were after *her,* and hoping at the same time that the Stranger had had start enough to escape them. When they asked her where he had gone, she said quite truly that she had no idea. They climbed around, but could find no trace, and at last they tramped away.

She noticed the name of the street now, for it was printed in golden letters on one of the buildings, *THE STREET OF GORGEOUS WISHES.*

She passed quickly by the next front. You could move pimples from outside your face to inside your kidneys by taking yellow *TRANSFER-TABLETS;* or hide a pain from yourself by a spoonful of *NERVE-NUMB;* or having worn out your heart or stomach, buy another. She wasn't quite clear about all this, and having never been sick, she found it of little interest.

In the next were men's clothes. It seemed they were made of something known as *MASCULON*. She read on a card:

A SUIT MOULDED OF MASCULON
FITS YOU INSIDE AS YOU REALLY ARE
LOOKS OUTSIDE AS YOU WANT TO LOOK
WHY SHOW YOURSELF AS YOU REALLY ARE?
YOU DON'T HAVE TO

This didn't seem right to her. "Why should you try to look like what you aren't?" she thought. "And what will people think of you when they find that you aren't what you look? . . . But I suppose that if everybody doesn't look as he really is, you always know that the person you are talking to is never the one you seem to be talking to, I mean the one you see in front of you . . . But how do you know who you are really talking to, for you never see him? . . . There is no sense in talking to someone's clothes, and it is hard to see who is hidden behind the windows and all the puffed-up suits they wear . . . So is anyone talking to anyone? . . . Dear me, this is too complicating altogether." So she smoothed her mind out, and went on to the next window which held her longer.

Here were shoes for ladies, made of some shiny stuff by the name of *SLEEK,* in reds and blacks, and close-fitting dresses made of a smooth cloth called *SKINTEX:*

MORE ENTICING TO THE HAND
THAN YOUR OWN SKIN
COMES IN
SHEER
SHEER SHEER
and
DISAPPEAR

Well, the dresses did look rather nice, she thought. She was just settling on which she liked best when a shadow fell, of something come between her and the sun. She flung around, and there just behind her was a metal claw, large enough, when down full, to grapple her against the clear wall. It had swung down from somewhere above, without a sound.

The claw stopped a thumb's width away. She made herself small, and watched it, frightened, feeling that if it were once to touch her she was caught. Looking down, she caught sight of her own dress. She had shorn the wool from the sheep's back, woven the cloth, dyed it, and sewn it herself. Maybe this was why she had always liked it . . . It had always kept her warm, too warm for this day perhaps . . . She ran her hands slowly down the skirt. It was a nice feel . . . Why had she suddenly wanted the shiny dresses? Her thoughts broke off here, for she saw the claw was gone. So quick and quiet. It was almost all folded back, in a slot above the front that she had not noticed.

She leant on the wall and sighed, heart still beating quickly. She stooped, intending to take her bag and go, but now her eye caught sight of the shoes. She noticed under the heel what looked like a short peg that must make the shoe hard to walk on, but apart from that, she thought she quite liked the colours of some of them. Then her muscles tensed. She remembered the claw. Her darting eye saw it come quietly down, though not so far as before, and then she ran away out of its reach as fast as ever she could. She stopped only when her breath was nearly gone, and she had reached another much larger square open to the sky, in the centre of which a very tall and wide building blocked her way. She stood at the foot of the tall tower she had seen from far away beyond the Fence.

The Golden Man

The front of the tower at street level was like a wide high mouth or deep cavern. What looked, from far away, like lower teeth were a row of white posts, and in front of each post stood a man. All the men wore suits, golden in colour, made, as Janey-Ann supposed, of Masculon. They were all the same in height, and looked, or else the suits made them look, exactly the same in width of chest, straightness of back, and levelness of shoulders. They wore hard round hats, and hard-looking gloves of the same colour, but no windows. She had not stayed long enough to have a good look at those who were chasing the Stranger, but now she was close to them.

"The Golden Men!" she said to herself. "The boy's father was right. They are still here. And I see the reason for the little windows. It's harder to say 'no' to a person you can't see. Or is it harder when you can see him? I don't know, but I still like to know when someone's in front of me, because what I say to him may depend on what I think of his looks."

High above each of the posts, at the top of the mouth was a large number printed on a white square, the whole row like a set of upper teeth. Above these numbers, right in the centre, was a painting of a large face, all complete except for the eyes, and where they ought to have been, were holes. Below it were two crossed arms, the hands open and held out, as if asking for something. The whole gave her the impression, when further away, of a skull and cross-bones; and she felt better to find that it wasn't.

Above this achievement were the words:

THE REPUBLIC OF FAIR-LOOK
GOVERNMENT HOUSE

and underneath, on a scroll made to look like a chain, was the motto:

WHAT SEEMS, IS — WHAT YOU GET, YOU ARE

She leant her head back, and at the very top, where the shiny trains of windows came closer together, up in the sky, was the dome she had seen last night, glowing white in the darkness. It seemed, like a fly's eye, to look down every way on the great city.

Janey-Ann wondered if this were a making-place where people worked. To ask, she was afraid; give an answer, she couldn't.

It was then that someone came from behind her, seized her arm, and asked her sternly why she was outside at such an hour. She turned her head and saw a Golden Man. He had one stripe on his cuff, which the men standing under the numbers didn't. His features were clear and sharp. He listened carefully to her; his words came quick when he spoke; but he didn't seem unkindly, so she made bold enough to say that she didn't know she was supposed to be anywhere. He took her to a little room at the corner of the mouth, sat her down, and looked at her curiously from ankle to neck. "Where did that get-up come from?" he asked her.

"You mean my dress?"

"Yes. I can't figure out what kind of machine would make that stuff."

"This," she answered curtly, holding up her hand, and turning it back to front several times.

"You're having me on," he said, unbelieving. "And what's in the bag?"

His curiosity made her hopeful. "They're seeds," she said. "They grow. Try some."

He nibbled one little seed, looked up at the ceiling as he savoured it, swallowed, thought about it, and said, "No. Definitely no. It tastes funny. No, I know what's wrong — it hasn't any taste at all."

"You mean you can't taste it," she retorted. "I can taste it; and grain is a good taste. After those knock-me-down flavours of yours, you aren't able to taste a nice gentle flavour any more."

"Listen!" the Golden Man answered. "I didn't ask you to give me any. You asked me to try them, and I've told you what I think. I'm not here to argue with you. You're here to be examined."

He rose and walked over to her, lifted her spreading pony-tail from her neck, and looked at it.

"Where are your wish-marks?" he asked in surprise.

"What are they?" she said.

"Come now. Did you never go at Kemmastime, and sit on Father Kem's empty chair, and tell him all you wished for, and have it printed on you."

"I've only just come here," she told him, "and why isn't Father Kem in his chair?"

"Don't change the subject. You passed all the shops along the street. Didn't you wish for something you saw there? Didn't the wish-printer print your wish with dye on the back of your neck?"

"You mean that horrid burny claw thing that comes down out of the air behind you?"

"You could describe it that way."

"Well, I think it was going to, but it changed its mind," she said.

The Golden Man scratched the hair on his temple. "I've never run into this before," he said. "Hmm."

He picked up a little Golden Book, turned the pages over till he found what he wanted. "Let me see. Here it is. 'Section one. Persons bearing wish-marks must comply strictly with all the following regulations.' That's what . . . "

Janey-Ann interrupted him: "You needn't go any further. There's at least one word there I don't know the meaning of."

"If you'll just let me finish my sentence," he said, "I'll make it clear enough even for you. No wish-marks, no rules. That means you can go. Now, now, not so fast," as she turned on her heel at once.

She turned back to him again.

"Just a word of advice. You get your hair cut."

"Oh, don't you like it?" said Janey-Ann.

"That's not the point. Wish-marks must be in full view at all times."

"But I haven't . . . " she began.

"I know you haven't any," he interrupted, rather sharply. "But how are we going to know if we can't see."

"But you said, wish-marks had to be in full view. That means that if you haven't any wish-marks, they mustn't be in full view."

"Look," he said, "we've got something better to do than stopping every girl we meet, and clearing all this hair away, just to see how many wish-marks she has — if any." He stressed the last two words, as if to head off any further argument.

"Now, that's strange. My brothers love messing my hair up," she said. "And anyway I'm the only one in the whole of Fair-Look, and you know all about me now . . ." And then she saw that for some reason he seemed to be getting cross, and suddenly she remembered the Green Boy. She thought, too, that it might be better not to tell the Golden Man that she hadn't the least intention of cutting her hair.

"Oh, this is where people work, isn't it? I know a boy who is working now. Would he be here?"

"Maybe. There are boys here. Too many. They tell the foreman how to run the place before they even know what it's for. And if they knew how to get their windows off, they'd be telling us too, I'm sure of that."

"He wears green."

"No good. What's his number?"

Luckily the boy had shown her the bracelet stamped with it, and he had written it on the back of her hand last night: "7373 stroke 44."

The Golden Man pressed a button and spoke the number into a square on the wall. Before she could say "Jack Robinson," a card had come up through a slit in his desk. He looked at it, and said, "Yes, he's here."

He reached over to drop the card into a large tube that rose out of the floor. He groaned a dismal "ah-h!" and straightened his back gingerly.

"What have you done?" Janey-Ann asked him with some concern.

He went over to a corner, stretched his arms to the ceiling, pressed something with his foot, and the top half of his golden uniform floated up and stuck to the ceiling, leaving him bare from the waist up.

"What have I done? Now that my jacket's off, have a look at what they've done! You see those marks," he shouted angrily. She did notice red sore spots wherever a bone showed through the skin.

"Nobody cares any more how he does his job, or how things go in this city, as long as they all get their wishes just when they want them. To take a mould of my body and make the jacket fit every bump on it, all they have to do is press a button. And what happens? It fits nowhere. And what will they say? Something's wrong with the computer. Well, what's wrong with the man that made the computer? What's wrong with the man that runs the computer? What's wrong with the man who sent me someone else's jacket? Instead of the jacket fitting me, it's grinding all my bumps down to make me fit the jacket.

"And it's not going to save them any trouble, for this is going back, and they're going to make me a new one. What's the use of clever machines when the people who use them are sloppy know-nothings? But let me tell you this — it doesn't happen round here. My men dress smart and do their work right — I see to that." He smiled grimly. "Here," — he took out of his drawer a cylinder with a button on top — "would you mind spraying this on wherever it looks sore. Just press the button."

She did so, and a blue liquid spread over the red. "Do you know what we could do?" she said. "If this blue comes off on the jacket, we might be able to mark the places where it needs changing — like putting pyjamas on to find out where you didn't dry yourself."

"It's not supposed to come off," he said.

"What's in this other jar? It's black sticky-looking stuff. That should make a mark."

"It should," he answered rather doubtfully. "But what if it glues the jacket on for the rest of my life? Well, just a little then."

He suffered into the jacket, and when he took it off again, they saw a strong black daub at every spot where the jacket made him sore. He was pleased about this, until suddenly he said, "But what am I going to wear? If I put the jacket back on, I'll never get it off."

"That's simple," she said. "Borrow one from one of the men at the posts, and then hide him away until he has to go home. Perhaps you can give him a pair of windows, then he won't be able to see himself. And now that that's disposed of, how do I find the boy?"

"It's not disposed of at all. You're sure there's nothing down the street you'd really like. You see, if you had just one wish-mark, I'd be quite sure the answer was, 'No, you can't.'"

She closed her eyes and shook her head fiercely, perhaps to shake the shoes out of her eyes. He sat at his desk.

"Pity. You know, I always feel more sure of myself when I say, 'No.' You never know what it'll lead to when you say, 'Yes .' "

He hesitated. "The book doesn't say much about persons bearing no wish-marks. There mustn't be very many of you." He closed his left eye, leant forward, and nodded confidentially. "You've got to be sure what you're doing on this job, or you don't hold it long." He reflected, and said reluctantly, "Well, if those with wish-marks can't do it, it looks to me as if those without wish-marks can. Stairway number six. Down you go."

"Thank you," she said, and ran to the door. She turned there and said, "You're a nice man," adding inside, "when you're not cross." She flicked her pony-tail to one side, and went out quickly, calling behind her, "I'm so glad you liked my dress and my long hair."

This annoyed him. She knew very well he hadn't said that. He sprang up, strode to the door, and threw it open. He felt the sun's warmth on his chest, and remembered he was bare from the waist up. He looked down, and saw a few of the black spots that covered him like a plague. And his eye caught one of his men coming towards him. He slammed the door, and locked it.

The making-place

Between every two posts, a stairway ran down into the earth. When she stepped on Stairway Number Six, she found the stairs were moving, very fast. She didn't have to step down them at all, but only to hold on to the hand-rail. Now the stair went straight, now in curves, and it must have travelled a long way before she landed abruptly in a huge round room.

For a moment she looked about her with astonishment. She couldn't have begun to describe it all. There were many long narrow roads whose tops were continuously moving along, and big boxes of all shapes and sizes lining each side of the roads, spewing things out on them, to be carried away. All wore, somewhere on them, round bright lights of red, green, or yellow, that kept going on and off, as if they were winking at her, like live things.

At the other side of the rows of boxes were walking lanes, and on either side of these lanes — and this, she thought, was the oddest thing in the room — people were seated on towers high up in the air. They weren't paying any attention to the machines below them, but were looking over the top of them to the tall wall of the room. Looking there, she could see coloured pictures of people moving; and, as far as she could make out, they were trying to kill one another. Now and then one of the people up on the high chairs would press his toe on something. He would then swivel round in his chair to look at another part of the wall.

Her first astonishment over, she quickly shrank back into the doorway. "I'm scared," she said to herself. "I don't know where to go — especially with all the people up there looking at me . . . But really, I'm not sure they are looking at me . . . As a matter of fact," — this was a little disappointing — "they're paying no attention to me at all . . . It would be silly to go back to the Golden Man, after he has let me come down here, and say I haven't been able to find the Green Boy . . . But where am I going to look for him? He might be anywhere."

The high chairs were each on a tall tower made of three thin pipes bound by criss-crosses. On each, at eye-level, was a white square. She tip-toed over to the nearest, and saw a number printed on it. "Well, that's a help," she thought. "That must be the number of the person at the top."

She thought of the boy's number. Suddenly giddy, she felt herself swept away at a tremendous speed. Then she found herself standing still in front of one of the towers. She collected herself for a moment, and saw that written on the white square was 7373/44.

Almost at once her attention was caught by the hissing and puffing of the nearest machine. It was long and white, and higher than she was. Running up each edge of its narrow front was a row of nuts, like buttons up a coat. On its top were two domes, like bald heads, she thought, and she remembered her uncle's saying that two heads were better than one, though she had never thought of both heads being on one person.

Halfway down the front of the machine, a little paw-like finger was moving over a picture drawn in black, lying on a ledge. Just above it, a chisel poking out from a large wheel was cutting exactly the same picture into a large slab the size of a table. She could tell this because, even though the slab was standing on its edge, she could see through it. In no time at all, the slab was cut, slid out on to the moving road and was carried away, and a blank slab fell down to take its place.

Janey-Ann had never seen a machine that almost looked and puffed and worked like a man. She wondered if the Giant looked like this. For a long time she stared in wonderment at the paws that felt and cut always exactly the same every time. At last she raised her eyes up to the two blind domes. She moved slowly backwards. It wasn't either man or Giant. It frightened her.

Ambion is persuaded

She looked up to the top of the tower, and there was the Green Boy, sitting on his high chair, looking straight ahead at the wall.

"What are you doing?" she called up.

"How did you get here?" he said in some amazement.

She replied as if it were nothing, "No trouble. A nice man with black spots told me where you were. But what are you doing up there? Why aren't you down here where everything's going on?"

"The machines don't need us, and work better without us — they say — so they stick us up here out of the way. They have to give us something to do, and I suppose someone has to look at the pictures they make."

"They could stop making them," she said.

"Right. But who's going to listen to you or me? And what would the picture-makers do? They wouldn't even have any pictures to watch. And what would I do then, all day? I can't eat all the time."

"If you don't do anything, why come?"

"If I don't come, I don't get paid. That machine's doing my job — the one that's cutting patterns in the plastic blocks. I used to like doing it. But it cuts them quicker, and always exactly the same each time. Except," added the Green Boy, "when it goes wacky."

"What does that mean?"

"Different things," he replied. "The other day, it kept cutting the same picture over and over again on the same piece of plastic."

"Why didn't you fix it?"

"Because I don't know how; and because it's none of my business; and because I enjoy watching how stupid it can be. They put it there instead of me: they can fix it." The Green Boy grinned.

"So they stop you doing work you like, and pay you to sit and watch pictures, not very nice ones, and ones you don't specially like even. I don't see that that's very clever."

"Oh people aren't clever here," he said. "It's the machines. And the cleverer they get, the stupider people get, but when stupid people run machines, machines can be stupid. And there's something about the pictures that keep you watching them, whether you like them or not. I suppose you come to like what you see all the time. And everyone here's the same. Everything we think we get from that wall. When I go to the Fence to look at the Tree-Land, it looks so different from what I see on the wall every day, I wonder if I could really live in such a strange place." He looked quickly down, smiling at her. "But since I've met you, I've begun again to think that that's where I must go." Then he frowned. "But how can I leave here with wish-marks?"

"It's something you think or do that gets you wish-marks; so there must be something else you can do to be rid of them. I'll try and find out what it is."

"I've never heard of anyone's crossing the Fence. How could I do it?"

Janey-Ann was annoyed. "Maybe they didn't try very hard. Do you want me to find out or not?"

"Oh yes, find out."

"Now, we'll need that whatever-it-is of yours with the two wheels . . ."

"The Galopede," he said.

"Yes. It must look as if you're just going home, or going for a ride, as you often do. We could even ride away from the Fence for a while, to fool the Golden Men." She stopped, and looked quickly round, to see if there were any Golden Men to hear her. She could see none.

"I know a road we can take," said the Green Boy. "It looks as if it goes back to the city, but it bends, after a while, the other way."

"Good," she said. "And remember that I am able to see the Golden Men, if any happen to be around."

"I don't know that I'd want to see them," said the

Green Boy, "but it might be useful."

She smiled. "It's been useful already. Stay here till I come back."

"Wait," he called after her. "We close up at fourteen hours. I'll see you outside at the stair top." She nodded, and was gone.

Arrested

Janey-Ann rushed back the way she came. The moving stairway carried her up, along, around, and up again at a great speed. She seemed as if aiming herself at a far dot of light, which suddenly started swelling faster and faster, till at last it was a huge white hoop of day, and leaping through it, she found herself between the posts at the top, where a hand in a golden glove came down from either side, and snatched her to a stop. A Golden Man at either side was looking at her, as if he had been waiting for her.

"And where do you think you're going?" said the man on the right.

He was the taller. His eyes and a small nose were clustered near the top of his face, with a wide mouth and a long jaw below them.

She looked up and down the long row of gates for the nice Golden Man with black spots who had let her go down, but he wasn't there. Perhaps he hadn't found a jacket yet. She hadn't thought of this. What should she do? Her earlier meetings with people here had made her bolder; she had the feel of the place now; she would face them down.

"I don't have to work, if that's the right word for it," she said, with the air of one who had lived in the place all her life. "I haven't any wish-marks."

Both grabbed the hair from the nape of her neck, and looked. Then they let it fall, and looked at one another over her head.

"Well, I'll be taxed," said the man who had spoken.

"We'll ship her," said the other.

"Where to?"

"The museum."

"Why?"

"Or the zoo."

"Why?"

"Or the hospital. That's best. She's a sick girl. They'll make her the same as everyone else."

The last speaker was shorter, his chin was lost in the round of his yellow puffy cheeks, his nose and lips were flat and heavy, and one eye was higher up than the other.

They hadn't given her a chance to ask their names, and they likely wouldn't tell her, she thought, they were so busy talking. She decided to call the last one who spoke "High-Eye," and the right name for the other couldn't be anything else but "Long-Jaw." Then she thought that if each grew interested enough in what the other was saying, they might forget about her. So she listened from one to the other with every appearance of eagerness, to encourage them as much as she could.

"But that's the point," said Long-Jaw. "She can't be different. It's impossible. Maybe the marks are not in the right place. Maybe she's rubbed them out." He fixed Janey-Ann with a severe eye. "And that's a pretty serious thing to do."

She met his gaze with an earnest look, as if appalled at the thought of such a thing, and murmured, "I'm sure it is."

High-Eye disagreed. "You're wrong there. The computer couldn't make a mistake like that, and she couldn't rub them out. It's more likely a poor lot of dye, and the colour has washed out. In which case," he added thoughtfully, "we might be able to spot the trace with a telescope."

"Microscope," said Long-Jaw, adding, in a friendly correction, the word that he knew High-Eye must have intended using.

"Or perhaps," said the other, considering it very carefully, "a periscope."

"Microscope," said Long-Jaw, a little more firmly.

"Or even, at a pinch, we might make do with a stethoscope."

Long-Jaw seized his hard hat, and slammed it down on the post beside him. "Microscope," he shouted.

"Don't give up," she pleaded, looking at High-Eye. "There must be another one."

There was a pause. She now noticed another Golden Man, who had three silver stripes on the cuff of his jacket, coming towards them, listening to the talk with a look of great interest.

"I don't think you're taking the matter seriously enough," said Long-Jaw.

"Me!" said High-Eye, looking at her, as if to back him up, though she wasn't quite sure how much he really meant it. He looked back at Long-Jaw, as one who could hardly believe his ears. "Who, up to now, is the only person who has put forward one idea after another for dealing with it? Not you. Not she — she hasn't been any help at all. And I have another one coming." He thought a moment. "By the Giant," he cried. "I know. It was in last week's puzzle. We'll use a kaleidoscope."

"What's that?" said Long-Jaw, disgruntled, adding suspiciously, "I think you're talking garbage."

There is no telling how long this might have gone on, for, as she found out later, there are all kinds of words ending in "-scope," and none of the things they stand for are any use at all for finding wish-marks, especially ones which aren't there. But at this moment, they both caught sight of the Golden Man with the three silver stripes, who had stopped quite close. Long-Jaw clapped his hard hat back on his head — it must have hurt him, she thought — and they both looked straight to their fronts.

She called the newcomer Silver-Stripes. (This, she thought, was the best name for him, for the other two certainly thought him a different kind of Golden Man from themselves, and the three stripes was the only difference she could see.) Her impression of him, indeed, was all of threes: the three stripes, three dark worry lines on his forehead, and three white fringes, one over each eye, and one under his nose.

He pushed out his lower lip. He closed his right eye and looked at Long-Jaw. He closed his left eye, and looked out of the other at High-Eye. He opened both eyes, poked his head forward, and looked at her. Then he looked at Long-Jaw, and raised the fringes over his eyes in a question.

"This female person, sir, was found breaking out of a making-place during working hours. Claims to have no marks. Pending investigation, we are holding her on a charge of skudekuveting."

"I didn't do any cutey-coveting, or whatever it is," said Janey-Ann, much offended. "I have never heard the word before, so how *could* I do it?"

Silver-Stripes also looked at the nape of her neck. He then beckoned her to come with him. This time the moving stairs went up and into the tall tower.

To the highest room

"So!" said Silver-Stripes thoughtfully, sitting down slowly, and looking up at her from under his fringes. "You've been skudekuveting."

"I'm sure I haven't," said Janey-Ann. "It doesn't sound like the sort of thing I would do; but it's really very hard for me to know, if I haven't heard the word before, and haven't any idea what it means."

Silver-Stripes reached for a Golden Book, and finding a particular page, chanted all on one breath and on one note: "Every one is guilty of skudekuveting who, having wish-marks, wilfully or negligently or in any other frame of mind, arrives at a making-place or leaves the same later than or earlier than the starting or ending respectively of the working period in such case made and provided by the Giant's Regulations for that person, thereby grievously discouraging other servants of the Giant."

He kissed the book and laid it down gently. "It's a

serious offence," he added. "Any offence in here," and he tapped the book with his right middle finger, "is serious."

"The words sound very serious indeed," said Janey-Ann, "but even if you had read them slowly and clearly, which you didn't always do, I counted five words I couldn't understand, and one of them was cosy-cosseting."

"That won't help you," he replied. "If we let everyone off who said he didn't know or couldn't understand the regulations, no one would do what he was supposed to do. The word is skudekuveting. It's not hard, if you say it slowly, *skew-du-cue-veting*."

"But how can people do what you want them to, if they don't know what it is?"

"But they do," said Silver-Stripes. "After every baby is born here, we lift a little flap of its head, and put a copy of this book inside."

Janey-Ann was appalled. "That big book in a baby's head?"

"Yes," he said. "But we put the book in a very cold room first, and shrink it down to the size of a pin head; and as he grows older, and looks around him, it all comes to him. But you seem to be strange here, so I'll tell you. Skudekuveting means getting something without working for it. What you get and what you give have got to balance up."

"Well, that settles it. I haven't got a single thing from

you — I don't want any. And you don't call that work down there, do you? Looking at pictures of people hurting one another? Any good Giant would want me to discourage them, as you said, from doing that. They might start doing what they see in the pictures."

"They have had their wishes, and if looking at pictures is what they have to do to pay for them, then that they must do," said Silver-Stripes.

"Maybe they don't like your pictures."

"Most people like them, and those who don't will have to put up with them. You can't make pictures for a few people who choose to be different. The more you give some people, the more they grouse."

"Most people here would look at anything," she said. "They wouldn't know the difference."

He didn't answer. He had left his seat. She spoke to his back, as he walked away from her across the room.

"Well, when they're going to sit and look at whatever's there, it ought to be something that'll make them nicer people. You have enough of the other kind here."

"Come over here," said Silver-Stripes. "We'll give you a few tests."

He took her over to a large dial on one wall, with little black ticks around its edge. She stood on a little ledge at the bottom of it, and he tied her to the dial by the waist. He went away and pressed a button, and she felt herself sticking to the dial, as if glued. The whole dial moved, tilting her head, which was near the top of it, ever so slightly to the right. He pressed another button, and she came unstuck.

She then lay on a table with a lighted band on the wall above it. Again he pressed a button, she heard a hum, and on the lighted band a little red something came flickering out slightly from one end.

"What's that all about?" she said, when she was on her feet again.

Silver-Stripes, at his table, calculating, said gravely, "You have point zero zero zero zero zero zero one of a wish-mark."

"I don't see how!" she said indignantly.

"Well, you must have eaten something lately."

"That stuff," she exclaimed. "That awful stuff! I hated it. I ought to get unwish marks for that."

"Well," he admitted, " your wish-mark has a half-life of only ten minutes."

"What does that mean?"

"It means, if I tried again, the machine might be able to find nothing."

"I should think so," she said. "A pig wouldn't eat it."

"There aren't any pigs here," he answered. "How do you know?"

"I am well acquainted with pigs," she said. "I have fed them nearly every day since I was a little girl. We have often spoken to one another, and it's something they feel very strongly about. If anyone knows what pigs like, I do."

All at once, a change came over Silver-Stripes. He rested his elbow on his desk, and his cheek on his hand, and he looked as though he were going to cry. "Why couldn't you have waited another ten minutes," he said.

"Why?" she asked, sorry for him, and wondering what was the matter.

"In ten minutes my watch is done, and someone else comes on; and if those two numskulls hadn't been so noisy, he'd have had to decide instead of me."

"About what?" she said, puzzled.

"I have never let anyone go before," he said, as if talking to himself. "And if I do, the fellow up above won't believe me when I say she has no wish-marks. If I take her up, so he can see, and ask him to decide, he'll say, 'What are you bothering me for? You know the rules. Make your own mind up.' And after I'm gone, he'll say, 'His sight's going, and his mind's going, and I think he'll have to go too.' I can see you have no wish-marks, and I know we shouldn't hold you; but he's a terrible fellow to deal with: no matter what you do, you're wrong."

Janey-Ann felt sorry for him. She let the matter soak a moment. "If the man on the floor above tells you what to do, who tells him what to do?"

"The man on the floor above him. But I can't go there. I can go only one floor higher."

"Has everyone got someone on the floor above him?"

"Right up to the Kemarch, and he has the Giant

above him," said Silver-Stripes.

"Well, suppose, instead of taking me up yourself, and getting into trouble — suppose I go up and see the Giant."

He pondered a bit, and spoke his thoughts again, "She won't have any wish-mark by now, so there really isn't anywhere she can't go."

"All right," said Janey-Ann. "If the Giant says I mayn't go, I'll come right back here to you. And if he says I may, they can't possibly blame you, can they? Now show me how to do it."

Silver-Stripes heaved a sigh. "I really don't see why it couldn't be done, and it would certainly help me," he said slowly. "Thank you."

He walked over to the wall and opened a door in it. Inside was a tiny room. "Stand there, and when I close the door, think of the person you wish to see, and the platform will stop at his floor. This lift will not go to the Giant, but only as far as the Kemarch. None of us has ever seen the Giant except him, and he is the only one who can take you to the Giant; but I don't think he can stop a person without wish-marks. Now step on the lift. Remember the word, Kemarch."

"Kemarch," she said.

"That's right," Silver-Stripes replied. "Good luck and thank you."

"Good-bye," she said with a smile, "and don't worry any more."

He closed the door. "Kemarch, Kemarch, Kemarch," Janey-Ann kept saying to herself. She felt herself soaring, to a soft continuous hissing, that now suddenly stopped ssssss-p, and all was quiet. Then she thought of Silver-Stripes again, and what he had told her.

She felt the lift falling. Then the hissing stopped again, ssssss-p.

"Now wasn't that silly of me," she said. "I must have been up there and then when I started thinking of Silver-Stripes again, down I went again to his place." She puckered up her brow, and put her mind only to Kemarch, Kemarch, Kemarch. Ssssss-p and silence once more. She saw no handle. She thrust at the wall, and it opened back, door-like. She stepped out and heaved a sigh; that had been a hard think.

The Kemarch

She was in a huge room, all the depth and width of the
building. Most of the wall, except where the lift came
up, was of the clear hard stuff she could see through.
Later, as she left the Kemarch's room, she passed close
to the wall, and looked out. She could see all the yellow
soil of the Giant's land, and, far away, the blue fringe of
the Tree-Land. So high was she above the streets below,
that the people she saw there — and she could see little
more than their heads — were like tiny round beetles,
restlessly moving, clustering in little troops and scuttling
apart again, though she couldn't make out that they
were doing anything. A spongy blue carpet covered all
the floor of the room; the ceilings and what there was of
solid wall were blue too.

In the very centre of the room was a huge black desk,
and at the farther side from her, a man sat. His hair was
grey, his suit — of the same design as the Golden Men's
— was black, with one golden bar on the cuff of the

sleeve. His eyes were black, and when their eyes met, she felt as though she were looking into a tunnel, dark and long.

His voice was calm and flowing, neither kind nor unkind, neither welcoming nor stern: "Why have you come to see me?"

"I should like to go home, sir," said Janey-Ann.

"And where is your home?"

"Over there among the trees."

"There is no reason why you should not. I can see by your face that you have no wish-marks."

"Down below they are not sure whether to let me go or not."

The Kemarch shrugged his shoulders, wrote something on a slip of paper, and gave it to her. "Show them this," he said.

"Thank you, sir," she said, and hesitated. "There's a boy who wants to come too."

"And is he a boy who belongs to Fair-Look, and has wish-marks?" He shook his head. "That is another matter. He must stay."

His firmness shattered hers, and left her unsure of herself. "Why can't he go if he wants to?"

"Does he want to? Does he want to — enough? Does he want other things more?"

Janey-Ann was silent.

"You are not unknown to me," said the Kemarch

further. "You entered Fair-Look in the late afternoon of yesterday. You met the boy you are interested in along the road, and you stayed with him and his father last night. This morning you had a conversation with a man who has given me considerable trouble, a man who, if he had his way, would make the people of the Giant unwilling to lead the well-provided, easy, satisfying lives they now do. He may think (and you likely think the same of the boy) that those he speaks to seek to lose their wish-marks. They really don't. And all who try to do without the gifts of the Giant only find they cannot. The people have made a good bargain; they have more things, and work less time and with less effort for them than ever before in this land. It is no service to them to make them discontented with what they have, and it upsets our time-tables."

"I liked the man," said Janey-Ann. She felt stubborn.

"So do I, and I know him far better than you," said the Kemarch, smiling. The smile went. "But no one can change him, and so I have to stop him; or else our whole way of life here, of making and using things, which, like a wheel, needs the flow of men's wishes to keep it moving, would come to an end."

"Well, sir," said Janey-Ann, "I want certain things too. Clothes like this. Water, milk. Sun-seeds. Why don't I have to work for you?"

"Because my factories don't make these. But he

whose factories do , has power to command you. That is a law."

"No one tells me what to do."

"What you mean is," said the Kemarch gently, "that you are not aware of anyone's telling you. Most people in Fair-Look think little of me or the Giant. They only know that they wish certain things, and only by doing certain work will they get them. Few of them see that people who wish less, work less; and have more time to live uncommanded by me or anyone else. And those who do see this have not the strength to cast their wishes from them. The young workman you are interested in does every day what I command him, and yet he hardly knows it is I who command, or even that I exist. Only you who look from outside can see this. And every day I give the things he wishes for."

"I don't think he does want what you give him," said Janey-Ann, feeling herself retreating before the Kemarch's power.

"That is not for you to say, but for him to prove," said the Kemarch. "I have been to the Fence; I have looked at the trees; I have thought how good a life one could live there."

"What stopped you?"

"The wish for this room was a stronger one," said the Kemarch. "It is a large room, and the highest in Fair-Look. I can see further from here than anyone else.

It is I who give orders; I take them from no one. These are my wish-marks. I would not forgo the trees for anything less. That is what is strange about the man you met. He too has given up the trees, but got nothing for himself."

This wasn't all clear to Janey-Ann, but one point she couldn't let pass: "Doesn't the Giant give you orders?"

"Yes. It is the Giant who says that all with wish-marks must stay in Fair-Look, and while they stay, they must work. I must give them what they wish, and in exchange for this, they are not free to do or think in certain ways, and must pay the tax when called upon."

"What does the Giant say about someone's going away?"

For a while the Kemarch said nothing. "Of the means by which a man may free himself and go," he said, "I know nothing. I have listened; but the Giant Kem-Erg has not spoken to me. Not everyone's ear can hear the Giant. It was the Kemarch sitting here before me who told me what it was the Giant commanded."

Janey-Ann still bore in mind what Silver-Stripes had told her ("I don't think he can stop you."). She pressed her lips together, breathed in deep, and said in a husky voice, "I want to see the Giant myself, sir."

"No one has seen the Giant," said the Kemarch slowly, "but I can't stop your trying. Come here."

He rose, and he stood a head taller than any of the

Golden Men, or those in the making-places. One of the Tall Men, she thought, of whom the boy had spoken. He lifted her onto the blotter that covered the centre of his desk. "Keep saying the Giant's name, and keep your mind on that only," he said.

"Kem-Erg. Kem-Erg. Kem-Erg," she kept saying.

The Giant

It was a room that glowed, but not from window or candle; it was a room somehow filled, and yet empty; it was a room of sounding silence. As in early dawn, there was light without sun, air without breeze, life without movement. The silence was fine as a spider's web, and she hardly dared breathe for fear it would shatter. It was ever so long before she remembered that what she had come for was to ask a question; and more time still before she gathered up the courage to ask it: "When I go, may the boy come too?"

The sound of the silence rose to the pitch of a soft flute, or a gentle wind in the trees. It was a sound that she had heard before. Where? It came to her mind: the voice of the Gate-Posts. And here was the voice again: "Wishes are the only bars; and they who abandon their wishes, break their bars."

"You mean that if he doesn't want Mish-Mash, or Masculon, or a Galopede, or things like that, he can go away from Fair - Look?"

"True," was the flute-like sound.

Once begun, she was now sure enough of herself to ask the question that had puzzled her, ever since the boy's father had spoken to her: "Why do you feed people that sawdust stuff, when you could grow them seeds and fruits, all of them tasting nice and all different? Why do you make them live and work underground? Why have you taken from them the smell of milk-weed and sweet clover? Why don't you stop them fighting and killing, instead of making it easier for them to do it?"

The answer came, but like words in a dream; she couldn't have said whether she heard them spoken or knew them some way else: "I am a Giant without hands or feet. Men are my hands and men my feet. Without man, my power would lie idle; men, without me, would perish of cold or hunger.

"Mish-Mash I make for those who wish it; and for those who wish sunseeds, I grow them. For those who love the earth and the life that thrives upon it, I make the trees that grasp it, streams that scrape grooves across its face, and all that swim and fly and run there; for those who scorn these, I throw on the wall images that please them, even if these at last harm or destroy them.

"It is my power that makes or destroys: it is men who choose what shall be made or destroyed. They have made me a shape with many taps, which pour out the many things they wish: if they left me without shape, wishing nothing, then might they come to know me as I am."

This led her to ask a third question: "Are you also the Giant of the Tree-Land, or have we another Giant over there?"

A low soft flute-like note rose high, whistled a while, and fell back into silence, like ripples dwindling. The silence lapped about her like a silken dream; but she wasn't one to stay quiet for long. "Well," she said, "I didn't understand it all, but I understand what I need to know now."

"And that makes you a very lucky girl," said the Kemarch, "for I have put questions many times, and been answered nothing."

"Thank you, sir," said Janey-Ann to the Kemarch, finding herself once again on the Kemarch's blotter.

Lazian

Janey-Ann had no further trouble going round, for all she had to do was show the Kemarch's note. She said to herself, "It really shouldn't make any difference at all; they should be able to see I have no wish-marks; but it does seem to help them see something, when someone important tells them what's there to see, or in my case, what isn't there. I must remember that from now on."

Out of the line of people pouring up Stairway Number Six, the Green Boy ran over to meet her. She told him all she had found out. "And all you have to do is to wipe out all those wish-marks. Oh, but they're big heavy ones," she finished up, looking at his neck.

"How do I do it?" he said, puzzled; but at that moment he saw, and beckoned over, a boy coming out of another stairway. His trousers were a washed-out blue, splotched with red paint, and frayed at the bottom, and a large eye was painted on the faded yellow chest of his droopy tunic. His tangled hair smelt of burlap, and was cut sharply off above his wish-marks. It seemed to her as she looked around that all the young people's legs were clad in tattered blue. "There were lots of nicer-coloured ones in the Street of Gorgeous Wishes," she thought, "and if all kinds of trousers cost them wish-marks, why would they wear the same as everyone else, and long after they ought to be used as floor-cloths? The Green Boy doesn't. The Golden Men must be making them do it."

"This is a friend of mine," said the Green Boy. "His name is Lazian, because he was born just before me. And this is Janey-Ann."

"Why is his name Lazian because he was born just before you?"

"We are not given a number until we start school," the Green Boy explained, "but when we are born we are given two consonants. We can add to them an ending and any vowels we like. His are *LZ* — that is, the end of the l's. And I am the first of the m's — *MB*. I could call myself Ambion, Mabian, Ombion, Mobien, or if I were a girl, Ambia, Embia, and all the rest."

"They even make your name up for you! I think it's none of their business."

Lazian wasn't like the Green Boy, she thought — more like the bright and brittle ones that passed her by on the Street of Gorgeous Wishes. She smiled, though, at a friend of the Green Boy. "Give him some sunseeds too, to see if he likes them."

Lazian chewed suspiciously. Then he stopped, squeezed up his nose as high as it would go, suddenly thrust out his tongue, and forcefully spat the seeds on the ground.

"You needn't have spat it out the way you did," she said sharply, hurt by this contempt for what she liked. "You could have been polite about it."

"Give me *NEW SCHLEE*," he said. His voice went up and down so evenly, that it was just as uninteresting as if he had spoken all on the same note, and he spoke fast, as if he had been given only a set time in which to get everything said. "I drank the whole of two jars last night. Better than *FLAVREX*. It's dear, of course. 'Satisfies but never fills, no matter how much you drink. Relax and be happy. Forget everything; like everyone. Take *SCHLEE* .'"

He snatched a tablet out of a pocket, threw it quickly into his mouth, and for the rest of their conversation, chewed it with gusto.

"I could forget this place, and most of its people," Janey-Ann remarked, "without any help at all."

She found herself watching his jaws, without specially wanting to, for each time he opened his mouth, he flipped from one place to another the little indestructible blob he was chewing. A cloud of some hard made-up smell poured out on his breath and enveloped all three, regardless of whether or not they liked it. She remembered a machine in the making-place, with a flap that kept opening and closing, down and up, dropping something out each time it opened. He looked much the same, she thought, but there was a difference: nothing useful ever came out of his mouth when it opened.

"I know we have to eat," she said to herself, "but if that's what I look like, I wouldn't want to be seen chewing more than I have to."

"If you don't like it here, why did you come?" Lazian demanded. "I know why. You came for the hep clothes, the great food, the gallop waggons we have here, to see the forgetters. You wouldn't catch our girls wearing stuff like that — who would look at them?" And from over his shoulder he ran a scornful eye from her bare feet to her head.

This hurt her. It was true the girls in Fair-Look did wear very bright colours. Their clothes were smooth to touch, and (though this she wasn't sure she liked) you could see through them. At home they said she wove well, but perhaps the Green Boy liked the cloth made without threads.

But he said, "I like her dress better; and she made it herself — that's more than our girls can do."

"So what?" said the Boy in Yellow. "Why make it when you can buy it?"

"But I would like to make things," the Green Boy said, "and they won't let me. What am I good for? Try the seeds again, Lazian."

"What are they anyway?" He spoke disdainfully.

Janey-Ann let the Green Boy tell him. "They're seeds. They grow on trees."

"Tree?" said Lazian. "What's a tree? Aw, don't bother. What do I have to know that for? And say — food doesn't grow anyway. Don't kid me. I know a guy that works where they make it. Don't tell me that."

The Green Boy spoke, upset. "I've seen trees. Away at the Fence. Like tall round pipes coming out of the earth, with bent branching cables that spread from the top, and shapes cut from green paper hanging from them."

"Oh well, if you've seen them, I'll believe you. Some of the things you say are way-out, but you get around. So what? Say there are trees — the seeds have no more taste than plastic waste, so what use are they? Why bother with them?" He narrowed his eyes, cocked his head, and chewed very slowly and quizzically. "Show me."

The Green Boy had caught the eye of Janey-Ann. He took the bag made of reeds from her. "I can't explain just now. I think it would take too long; but take the seeds with you. Try them again. Try to like them, Lazian. And if I can, I'll see you later on."

Lazian shrugged. His jaws began chopping again with a slosh of cascading saliva. "O.K.," he said, took the bag with what was left of the sunseeds, and off he went, chin up, swaying side to side with each long stride, pleased with himself at putting the Green Boy down.

Just then he caught sight of a girl, and ran towards her. Above the smooth pale blue of her trousers, on the tail of her glossy yellow jacket, she had sewn an eye, black and white, like Lazian's. Her straw-coloured hair was just long enough to cover her ears.

"That girl of his," she said to the Green Boy. "Is it because of what she's wearing that he likes her? What's so wonderful about it? It's frayed, it's stained, it's faded and it's patched. It's the same as nearly everyone else's working here. Where I live, they'd use it to wipe the horses down, long before it looked as bad as that."

"I wish I were as sure of everything as he is," the Green Boy said, as if he were envious.

"You can be sure, and still be wrong," said Janey-Ann, in the tone of one quite sure she was right.

Lazian had flung his arms and the bag around the girl, and spent some time kissing her. He took something from his pocket, threw the wrapper on the ground, and poked the contents into her mouth. They walked away, Lazian's arm around the girl's waist, and his head bent round under hers, and looking up at her. The Green Boy, who looked after the two with troubled face, was quite forgotten.

Janey-Ann could see he was fond of Lazian, so she waited a moment before she went up to where he stood, and said softly, "Look how long our shadows are; and the trees are so far away we can't see them."

He turned with a sudden smile. "We won't ride yet,"

he said. "We shan't be noticed quite as much, if we move at the same pace as all these other people."

Walking down the street, she noticed the boy's eyes, though now and then he tugged them back, reading the wide shop fronts and what they urged him to buy. She was afraid for him. But near the door of one shop, the eyes of both fell to the white walk. Lying on its side was a reed bag, and splayed from its mouth was a splash of sunseeds. The feet of the passers-by trod over the seeds and round the bag, until, as they watched, a man kicked the bag out of his way towards the wall. Janey-Ann's glance rose to the shop-front:

NEW
BETTER
SCHLEE
ECSTATIC — EXOTIC — EXHILARATING
with handy nipple

He looked up. "We'll ride now," he said. As she sat behind him on the Galopede, she saw that one of the wish-marks was much fainter.

A parting

The Green Boy stopped the Galopede. They were at the edge of the city, in front of a doorway. She had been to the house only once before, and the entrances to all the houses looked the same: but she knew which one it must be. They looked ahead. The Tree-Land was a band of tiny trees, a long hazy blue cloud between earth and sky.

Without a word, they dismounted from the Galopede, and he laid it on the ground. The boy said, "I must see my father." She nodded, and watched his back as he went in. She didn't think the father would stop his going, but the boy was fond of his father, and mightn't wish to leave him.

She swung full round, faced the city, and raised her eye up the tower to the Kemarch's gleaming dome. There was the other question. Was the Kemarch watching? She lowered her eyes to the street again, where still some people passed and re-passed. She kept her eye on some of them. A dark man with a bag went into one of the houses, and came out again empty-handed; a girl in blue had been standing across the street, and started off in a hurry towards the tall tower; two men at the corner, with books under their arms, were talking all the time till the boy came back. Were some of these they that watched for the Kemarch?

" . . . Yes," his father said, "that was many years ago. Never again have I looked across the Fence of Unwish and watched the trees. It was easier not to think of them at all." He shrugged. "My girl — your mother — liked the red streets here, their shows and fads, their sham food, their easy ways for the impatient, more than the cool deep woods and clovery pastures . . . But must you go at once?"

After a pause the Green Boy said, "I think that what I don't do now, I shall never do. She told me that, and I think she is right. And it is growing late."

"She is right," his father said, "and if I have not said to you all I should have said in all the years we have been together, it's much too late to say it now."

"You are going to be lonely, living here by yourself. Couldn't you come with us?" the Green Boy asked him. "Your wish-marks — "

"Wish-marks," his father interrupted, "as a man grows older, are harder to be rid of. For me it is not a possibility; for you it is."

The Green Boy sat on the floor by his father's chair . . . The shadow cast by the Galopede had stretched much farther when he came above ground again and lifted it. They both mounted, and rode past the last house without speaking.

A paper blows away

"We shall take this road," said the Green Boy, pointing along one which led at a right angle to the one they were on, the one by which Janey-Ann had come from the Tree-Land. "If anyone is watching, it won't seem as if we were going to the Tree-Land; but out near the quarry, the road curves back near to the one we are on, and we can strike back to it again across country, out there where I am sure there is no one to see us."

Janey-Ann nodded agreement.

They rode along, as fast as the Galopede could go, and after awhile Janey-Ann became aware of a noise that kept growing louder and louder — about a dozen short grunts, followed by a long sniff — like a dragon breathing, she thought. As they rose up over the top of a knoll, and began wheeling faster down the other side, she saw what was making the noise.

She saw a quarry, long, deep and wide. If you had planted the Kemarch's tower in it, its dome would not have reached the brow. The floor of the valley, far down, was like a doll's world — tiny roads, little hills, a square dot of a house, and a speck, that seemed hardly to move, that the Green Boy said was a man walking.

The dragon-breathing came from a square tube at the edge of the quarry. As it went sliding down a tall post, it must have eaten up the earth below it, for when it swooped up the post again, sniffing, the earth where it had gone down wasn't there any more. Each time it came up, it moved sideways, eating a ledge along the wall of the quarry. All the way down to the foot of the slope, other machines were eating other ledges, and in this way the quarry was growing longer all the time. The place was so loud with grunting and sniffing, that it sounded like a zoo of dragons, and she and the boy could hardly hear what the other said.

And the fierce gusty wind, which had tousled her first when she entered Fair-Look, made hearing harder still. Gentler between houses, here where no house rose in the wide sweep of weather-sculptured clay, the roaring pouring air never ceased.

It was a disturbing place: wind lashed their hair and clothes, a hail of sound beat upon them, the huge tubes pounded ceaselessly to swallow up the earth on which they were standing; and there was no one there. It was as if someone had started it all a long time ago, had left, and forgotten about it; as if no one really cared any more what was going to happen.

The pocket of her skirt was very small, where she had placed the Kemarch's useful slip of paper that said she had no wish-marks. It must have been sticking out a little, because, as she went near the edge of the quarry, the wind whipped it out of her pocket, and blew it over on to the top terrace. She mustn't lose that. She must get it before it was blown again, down into the quarry where she couldn't find it. She ran to the edge. The Green Boy shouted, but she didn't hear him, and before he could stop her, she had started climbing down. The side was crumbly, and she slithered more than climbed, threw herself on the paper, and put it back again, pressed well down to the bottom of her pocket.

But when she tried climbing up again, the side kept crumbling down, every time she clutched at it. The Green Boy lay on his chest, and reached, but he was at the top and she was always at the bottom, however many times she dug her toes and fingers into the earth.

Suddenly he sprang to his feet, and ran along to where the dragon was going up, sniffing. There was a wide step at the bottom of the tube. He leapt on to the step, and steadied himself by gripping a metal bar that came out of the tube at shoulder level — just before the tube went grunting down. The tube, and the boy, shook, as it ate its way down. At the bottom he made a sign to Janey-Ann to jump on when it came down again. The tube hoisted him up, and he leapt off at the top. When it reached the bottom again, Janey-Ann jumped quickly on to the step, and grabbed the bar. The Green Boy took her hand, and helped her off at the top. As she leapt, the sniffing stopped, and the tube stood still.

"What did you do?" the Green Boy shouted.

"Nothing that I know of," she answered.

The Green Boy looked carefully at the tube. "That bar we were holding. It used to be straight up. Now it's sideways. I'll try pushing it back the way it was."

He stood on the step and pushed the bar up, and at once the tube started sniffing again. He jumped off just as the grunting began. He caught her hand, they started running back to the Galopede, got on, and made off as fast as they could.

When they were far enough away to hear one another, Janey-Ann asked him, "What happens to all the earth that's gobbled up?"

"It goes through a pipe to the making-places, where they mix it or melt it down into all kinds of things. I thought we had better leave that place as fast as possible. The machines don't need men to run them, but when a machine stops, as that one did, a red light goes on somewhere, and a man comes to see what has happened, and I didn't want him to see us."

"You know," said Janey-Ann, "I wasn't really thinking what I was doing. I don't really need a paper telling me what I know, or telling other people what they can see for themselves. That paper doesn't make anything different. If I lose it again, I won't go after it, or, before I know it, I'll be getting wish-marks for a piece of paper saying I haven't any." They both laughed.

Over the edge

The road was now turning towards the Fence and the other road that would take them there. The grunting and sniffing could now hardly be heard, covered over by another sound that was growing louder, a steady pounding. The huge quarry had curved away from the road, and across it she could see a great bridge. On the bridge was a little house, and up and down through the little house, the handle of a tremendous hammer rose up slowly, and slammed rapidly down, the huge head at the bottom of the handle pounding down on a mass of things that nearly filled that part of the quarry.

Along the edge of the quarry, a number of big waggons were moving, and something she couldn't see was pushing what was on the waggons down into the valley. One of them carried what looked like half a house, another bore machines like those she had seen in the making-place, and a number held huge boxes, one wall of which was lifted up, and a torrent of little things spewed out and down the quarry wall. And all the while the great hammer kept crunching down, packing them all tight.

"Those are things we've stopped using," the Green Boy said.

"It's an awful lot," said Janey-Ann. "It's filled up a long way back. Surely things last longer than that."

"They don't let us use things more than two years. It used to be ten, but they keep making it less. Things are made so quickly now, we couldn't use them all up unless we threw them out sooner. They blow our houses up every four years, and build us new ones. I wish they wouldn't: the first house I remember living in was much nicer than what we have now."

"And it's a silly thing to do," Janey-Ann added. "If you keep on that way, you'll end up using everything once. Imagine using knives and forks and spoons and cups only once, and then throwing them out. What a waste that would be! Imagine using a house for a day, and then breaking it up!"

They laughed. "No," he said, "I can't imagine that."

"You needn't laugh," she said. "You said yourself you use your houses only four years. Soon it'll be three and then two. My uncle told me that in dry places where little grows, and people have to walk a long way to find food, they build little houses and live in them for only a day or two. They make them of branches and leaves. You may be doing the same, building a new house every day. And, after we're dead, how will people know that you and I ever lived if we can't leave them something we liked or used. A cup we drank from, or a letter we wrote, or maybe a book. I have a cup like that, and whenever I use it, I think of the girl who drank from it long before I was born. It's so exciting to think of someone living so long ago, and yet so like me. Or maybe it's the way she is not like me that's exciting. I'm not sure. Both, I think. She's like me, and she isn't like me."

He shook his head. "All books over a month old are picked up, and the paper used again. Books over a month old aren't relevant, they say, whatever that means. But look at this." He looked around him cautiously before he brought something out of his pocket, and showed it to her. "I'm not supposed to keep this, but it's a pocket knife my father gave me once, that his father used." The handle was dark brown, but the blade, when the boy unfolded it, shone in the sun. "You can sharpen this, you know," he said, "when it grows blunt."

"Why not?" she said.

"You can't sharpen the new ones," he explained. "You throw them away when they're blunt, and buy another."

"And what a mess it is," she said, walking to the edge of the quarry for a last look. "How many of these big holes have you?"

"About a hundred," he said, "but now they're filling them faster, and soon there'll be more."

She looked into the quarry. "It's like a disease," she said, "eating the land away. Some day all your land will look like this. Some day — there must be a day — there won't be any left. What will you do then?"

The rough wind had spread a haze of dusty soil through all the air, and even things just below were pale and bleached. The quarry wall was a long slope, with streaks, as if someone had brushed it from top to bottom. The foot of the slope was darker: the boy said it was the bigger, heavier pieces, and showed her little streams flowing down the slope all the time, and once and again a large pebble breaking out from its place, and tearing down the slope in a straight line, to stop suddenly far, far below.

She leant forward and peered through the haze, to make out something across the valley she thought was moving. There was a wild gust of wind from behind her, and she felt as if hands had lifted her up and dropped her down again out on the loose soil of the slope, which slithered easily downwards, and her with it. She threw her arms up to avoid pitching forward, and fell flat on her back. For the time being she stopped sliding, but she hardly dared breathe for fear it might start her off again.

"Don't move," the Green Boy shouted.

Even with both stretching hard, he couldn't reach her.

"Hold on: stay still," he said. "I'll find something."

He looked round. All he could see was the Galopede. He looked at it. At the tires. He took out his grandfather's knife. If his wish-marks were to go, he knew he must leave the Galopede behind; but he had been keeping the thought of losing it at the back of his mind: it was something to think about later on — he could leave it at the Fence. But now he had to think about it. He could cut the tires off the rims, and make them into a kind of rope. He unfolded the knife. If he cut the tire, that would be the end of the Galopede; and he had given up so many things to get it; and it was a faster way to reach the Fence than walking. It was one way he was different, for not many others bought Galopedes; and he liked running it: he felt he knew how to make it do whatever he wished.

"I'm sliding further down." It was Janey-Ann calling to him. He had forgotten her for the moment.

"I won't be long," he shouted. It came to him suddenly that if he couldn't pull Janey-Ann back to the top, and pretty soon, he would lose her, and that if he had to choose between her and the Galopede, it must be she. Even if she did slide to the bottom without hurt, without setting a landslide off and being buried, by the time he had found a way down, and both of them had found a way up, they would almost certainly be found by the Golden Men. They had spent too long here now. And he would be kept, and she would have to go home.

The tire was tougher than he thought, and longer cutting. When both tires were off the rims, he slit each of them in two, and then tied the four pieces together. He lay down at the edge, and leaning over as far as he dared, he wiggled the end down to Janey-Ann. The tire tossed sand into her hair, and once he thought he had started a flow of sand and had to stop. At last she caught it with both her hands, and he pulled up slowly, afraid that one of the clumsy knots would give.

She tried pushing down with her feet and one hand: the sand went down, but she stayed where she was. When he had pulled her halfway to the top, the middle knot suddenly sprang out, and the rope was in two pieces. By now she was close enough that he could reach and seize her half of the rope, and little by little brought her up to where he could seize her hands, and tug her over the brink.

"Thank you, Green Boy," she said. "If I had slid down there, it would have taken days to get out."

"You mightn't have got out," said the Green Boy seriously. "You might have started a landslide as you went down, and been buried in it."

"It was a stupid thing to do." She was still frightened; but also a little vexed, for she had thought of herself as a sensible person who didn't do stupid things. "I hope no one saw me. They might think you were throwing away a person you didn't want; and that would be a nasty idea to put into their heads. We'd better go away from here as fast as we can, before I do something even worse."

They turned their backs on the quarry. Without its tires, the Galopede bumped and clattered over the bare, lumpy, rock-like earth. Until they reached the road that would lead them to the trees, it was easier to walk it than ride it.

Janey-Ann stopped. "You know, it felt as if someone lifted and threw me over . . . If I wasn't so sure I could always see the Golden Men . . . but I wouldn't have seen one standing behind me . . ."

"Yes?" said the Green Boy.

"Do you suppose," she said, "that one of them could have pushed me over the edge?"

The face beyond the grille

They had reached the road, and were riding straight for
the Fence. There were still wish-marks on the boy's
neck, fainter, but still to be seen. Still and again, she
kept looking back, but the road was always empty. It
made her uneasy. The Kemarch was a clever man, and
he knew nearly everything. He must know that the boy
was leaving and still had wish-marks. What was he
doing about it?

Now in the open country, all that was near the road
was the line of little metal houses, twice as high as she
was, and the whole of the side that faced away from the
road covered with a screen or grille. The Green Boy said
they were not houses, but the tops of shafts or chimneys
by which air was taken underground for the making-
places.

They came to the one that had the stone in front,
where she had met the Green Boy. They stopped the
Galopede, and with one accord walked over the hard

earth to the sitting stone. They sat and thought of what their meeting had brought, less than a day, but many changes ago. Green Boy's excitement was damped by weariness. She thought he might be thinking of his father. It was hard to know what to say. She was going home, but he was leaving all that had been home to him since childhood. She was much less sure than she had been that it stood with kindness to urge the boy so strongly to leave the City with her.

They had not been able to use the Galopede in open country, but even though it was bumpy without its tires, they felt they must ride it along the road, because of time. They decided to make one stop here, and one more at the bridge, to see the tree; that was all, and they would make them short.

"I think I'll put the Galopede where it can't be seen from the road," the boy said to her. "Just in case. We're safer off the road, for if they come looking for us, we couldn't get off the pavement quickly enough. Let's hope they come while we're here."

Her eye searched the waste of yellow earth, but always came back to the road from the city, the strangely empty road. "Why is it that nothing grows here," she asked.

"Because they kill it," he said, suddenly angry. "They spray it with 2D, one of their poisons. They've got a poison for everything, even for people. That's right. They have a 7D they kill people with when they're fighting." He was quiet again. "You grow things: all we do here is destroy."

"Good," she was saying to herself, "he really does want to go," when she was startled by the boy's grabbing her by the hand, and pulling her to the side of the house away from the City.

"Quick," he cried.

As a gallop-waggon hissed past at great speed, they slipped round the corner to the back of the box away from the road, where the grille was. Though the row of little houses kept them from seeing it, they kept looking the way the waggon had gone, till they could hear it no more, and then they looked at one another.

Suddenly her heart thumped, as if to leap from her chest. Something had caught her eye. She turned. Looking at them through the grille was a face.

The Stranger advises

"So it's you they're after," said the face. "I thought it might be me." She saw it was the Stranger. Her taut muscles relaxed as she sank against the wires of the grille and smiled.

"It's all right," she said to the Green Boy, "this is the Stranger I told you about. We are running away from the Kemarch," she went on, turning to the Stranger, "and Green Boy is coming to the trees with me."

"A good place to go to," the Stranger said, "and a good man to run away from. If you don't, he'll have you doing whatever he tells you to, every waking moment. For he is good at his job — he's a better man than the muddleheads that work for him. But come in, till the gallop-waggon passes on its way back. It won't be long, but it won't be safe to go on, until it has passed."

To their surprise, he opened out the grille to let them in, led them down a dozen rungs or so of a ladder that went on down the shaft, and then into a little cave in the side of it, where he lit a candle. Three posts along each side, and the beams across their tops, had been cut from trees and held up the roof. Thin straight boughs ran above and between the beams like a ceiling, and kept the earth from falling. The door of the cave was a single square sheet of the metal that lined the shaft, and when it was shut, it looked no different at all from the rest of the wall, and you wouldn't have said there was a door there at all.

As they went inside, "Where did you get the wood for your little room?" Janey-Ann inquired of the Stranger.

"It all had to come from across the Fence — by night, between the Golden Men's patrols. I cannot use things from the Kemarch's realm — that would be dangerous."

"I've heard about you," said the boy. "They call you a Leveller. They say you want to take everything from us, so none of us will have any more than you. It would be pretty hard for us to live like that — for them, I mean. I think I might. They tell us to catch you and have you taxed."

"Do I look like a man who does, or would, or could, take things from you? Do you see much booty down here? Taking things from you wouldn't help you, so long as you keep on wishing for them, for the things we desire are like huge heavy packs upon our backs, whether we have them or not." He laughed ruefully. "The Kemarch is the man who puts the pack there. He even steals your thoughts, and puts the ones he wants in place of them. And instead of your hating him for doing this to you, he finds it handy to have you hating me. A clever, clever man."

They sat on a wooden bench along the side of the cave. He opened a box at the end of the bench, and offered them sunseeds, dried apples, and water. They were hungry. The Stranger went up to keep watch at the grille.

"Lucky for me the traffic isn't heavy up and down chimneys," he said. "One man a year or so, but I'm out early and in late, so I've never met him. It's just as well. I hope I never do. You'd think I'd have a wish-mark for a nice quiet front hall like that out there, even though it is an odd shape, a private place all to myself, and the hum below just loud enough to drown my noise. What saves me, of course, is that, so far as they're concerned, it isn't a front hall, and most of the time, they pretend I don't exist. So how can they put a wish-mark on a person who doesn't exist for a place which doesn't exist. That's going too far, even for them — who spend their lives pretending." And they heard him laugh.

He was still speaking down from the top of the shaft. "Coming back, they pass on this side of the ventilators, to make sure no one hides behind as you did. They count on taking you by surprise, they come so fast. The patrol will pass here on its way back in fifteen minutes. It ought to, but doesn't, occur to them that people will notice that every day they do exactly the same. It is queer too that they never seem to suspect that the stone you sat on is the mark by which I pick my ventilator out from all the others."

He stopped; and the only sound was the distant continuous hum from underground. He must have been listening.

"Here is a piece of counsel I should give you: whether or not the Kemarch's men spy you out before you reach the Fence, the young man will not be able to find a way through it, as long as those wish-marks can be seen; and if he doesn't find a way through before long, they will certainly catch him. Others besides you have sat on the stone — but few have passed the Fence."

"What can I do?" said the boy, helplessly. "I've left everything behind. I have nothing any more but what I have on me."

"It's not enough to give something away, and go on wanting it."

"I can throw something away that's in my hand," the boy said, "but how do you throw a wish away?"

"No," said the Stranger. "You can't go at it that way. But some time, another wish must grow — perhaps in a sudden moment — so much stronger than the one that's there, that it ousts it from its place, and sits there instead; and the wish-mark will vanish as the wish does; for the wishes that leave marks are for the things the Kemarch makes."

There was quiet for a while, except for the hum from below. Janey-Ann and the boy were eating in the cave, and the Stranger was listening at the grille. Then the boy said, "Janey-Ann, can you walk from here to the Fence?"

"I walked it yesterday," she said.

"We can travel faster, if I wrap your feet in something."

"I suppose so," she said. "Why do you ask?"

He called out to the Stranger, "Can we leave the Galopede with you?"

"I don't want it," said the Stranger. "I might be tempted to use it, and then the Kemarch would have me. But I can find a place to hide it, and it might be of use to someone else, escaping like yourselves. But won't you need it?"

"I think," said the boy, "I need to be rid of it. I can see that I'm too fond of it. It'll be easier to reach the trees without it than with it. I just wish I had used it more when I did have it."

"You are quite right," said the Stranger.

"That was well done, Green Boy," said Janey-Ann. She turned his head and cried out, "A wish-mark has nearly gone, and the others are fainter."

A strong rising whistle grew louder, blasted into the shaft, and then grew less into the distance. Janey-Ann and the Green Boy doused the candle, and ran to the door of the cave.

"Now," said the Stranger, rising up from below the grille, having ducked when the waggon passed. "Stay off the road, and walk along behind the ventilating chimneys, or, as Janey-Ann likes to call them, little houses." He smiled at her. "You have almost exactly an hour. You should be able to reach the ditch by then. Hide under the bridge till you hear them pass. From there on, leave the road, and follow the side of the stream, keeping your heads below the top of the bank; and when the stream is nearest the Fence, make a run for it."

To the boy he said, "If anyone can pass the Fence, you can. You are in good hands." To Janey-Ann, he said, "Help him all you can." He gave them each a hand. "Good-bye, friends. Good fortune."

Janey-Ann returns

The sun was closing down to a stern sea of purple, with flaming spray hurled into the glowing air above, as they reached the ditch.

The road kept on over the ditch by a bridge. This was the bridge beside which Janey-Ann had planted her Trembling Aspen. They left the road, and ran down the grey sandy bank to where it was. Even in the dusk it was easy to find, for it rose alone in the long and grey waste that sloped from the yellow plain to the pale chalky waters. Even in a day, the leaves had gone black. They stood by it a moment, looking down, and then walked over to the bridge, to sit under it on the sand, and lean against the pier that held it up.

"If that tree were grown up," she said, "we could tell if it's going to rain; for if it is, the leaves curl up, and all you can see is the pale underneath. The whole tree changes colour."

"I didn't know that," said the Green Boy, "but I

would climb it, and see what the world looks like to a tree."

"Do you know they say," Janey-Ann went on, "that if you pin a lock of your hair to an aspen, and say, 'Aspen tree, aspen tree, prithee shake instead of me,' and say nothing else until you get home, it will cure you of an ague, because it trembles, and you tremble too when you have an ague. Oh, there are so many stories told of trees. My uncle has a great big book, and every night he reads to us from it, and I try to remember all it says about the trees. One queer thing was, 'I see men as trees walking.' Wouldn't it be strange to see a tree walking — how could it walk with only one foot — for that's all a root is — just one foot. It could only hop, and that would look even stranger."

"And they'd have to hop in rivers, to get water," the boy said. "What a splash that would be!" And they laughed.

"Some have lots of snaky roots. They might creep along. Another thing I liked was, 'All the trees of the field shall clap their hands.' Now I can see that, for sometimes, when their branches move together, it is almost clapping."

"I like that," said the Green Boy, "for it helps me to feel how trees feel. I am sure trees can be happy, just as we can. That's an interesting book. What is its name?"

"It's called *The Book,* and it was written over two thousand years ago — not one month only, like yours."

"I've never heard of that book, and I read more books than most boys. I am sure no one else here has read it."

"Well," she said with a smile, "once we're safe across the Fence, we'll read it together. It's because of the book, you see, that I planted the aspen here. Someone was like a tree planted by the water, and spreading out her roots, 'and her leaf shall be green.' So I planted it here: and you see what happened."

She sighed. After a silence, her eyes rose to his face. She looked at his eyes for a while.

"I wish you would take those windows off," she said, now very serious.

"I'm afraid to," he said. "I don't want to see the Golden Men. And there may be other things . . ."

"Nor will you see the gold that I shall see, Green Boy, on the leaves when the sun shines; the golden ground in autumn, the golden clouds, the golden glitter of river pebbles."

He looked at her, torn in two. "I can't," he said. "If I took them off, I shouldn't be able to put them back on. Only they can do that, so they'd know I had them off."

"You won't need them any more."

"How can I be sure?"

"Nothing is sure, Green Boy," she said. "I don't know there is going to be a Gate, when we reach the Fence." She stood and looked over the edge of the ditch at the Fence, and the trees that now rose tall beyond it. "But I don't belong in that city of yours. I can't live there. So whether there is a Gate or not, I have to walk back towards the trees."

This was when they heard again the rising whistle shriek out of the distance, hiss over the bridge above them, and sink back into the quiet it had leapt out of.

The boy stood. "Come," he said. "The Suers are on the move. They are the Golden Men that hunt escapers like us. So we must move too. I know where the ditch is nearest the Fence."

Their heads were well below the floor of the plain, for the stream had flushed a deep gully in it. The road, which up till now drove in a straight line towards the trees, bent in order to run in line with the Fence, and thus crossed the stream again by another bridge. On reaching this bridge, they crawled up to the brow of the slope, and looked cautiously over. "There," she said, pointing from where they lay, straight to the Fence, "there is where the Gate was." But in the growing dark, their eyes could not be sure if Gate there now were. The road running straight in line with the Fence was empty. A white light shone in the Kemarch's dome. Did he know?

They rose, and over the gully's brow made for the Fence. They were no more than a third of the way, when looking back, they saw a pair of lights hastening toward them along the darkening road, and a broad beam of light swept the Fence and the land between it and the road, where the two of them were.

"Green Boy," she said, "we must run."

They ran indeed. The Fence was near enough now, that she could see a Gate, and it was open. "Do you see the Gate, Green Boy," she cried in delight. "Faster."

"There is no Gate, only Fence," he breathed, panting.

"Pull your shoes off," she cried. He looked at her, wondering; but stopped, pulled them off, grabbed them in his hand, and ran again.

"Throw them away," she cried.

He stopped, looked round at the approaching lights, threw the shoes away, and cried "Lie down."

They threw themselves on the ground, and the wide glaring beam flashed over where they lay. It passed, halted, swept back, and stayed full upon them.

"My breath is gone," he said. "I can run no more."

"Is that a purse at your belt," she said, "with rocks in it to buy things with?"

"Yes."

"Throw it away."

He unstrapped it, and left it on the ground. She took his hand. "Now," she said, "as fast as you can." They rose and ran again; though not a step could he have run, but for the touch of her hand, that somehow lifted weight off his feet, which he felt hardly grazed the ground as he went.

"Can you see a Gate?" she cried.

"There is no Gate," he answered, gasping.

Janey-Ann looked over her shoulder. The gallop-waggon had stopped at the bridge. Seven Golden Men from it were running after them. The Fence was only seven or eight waggon lengths ahead. Each time the Green Boy had thrown something away, his wish-marks had been dimmer. Still there was a trace. Each time he had thrown something away, he had run faster.

"Throw off your coat," she cried.

He ripped it off, and flung it behind him. Footsteps were thudding close. To look to see how close they did not dare.

Tall trees reached arms above them, as if to receive them. A hand gripped the Green Boy's arm. It swung him round. His head fell back and struck the Fence. It struck so hard the windows fell from his eyes. Above him he saw the tiny black discs of an aspen twinkling serenely against the failing blue, and, glittering in and out, the first golden star of dusk. The tiny seedling dead in the grey sand came back to his eyes.

"Take him for the tax," a harsh voice commanded.

He looked down, to the grip that held his arm — then to the Golden Man he saw had seized it, the first Golden Man he had ever seen.

"No," he shouted, and wrenched his arm free.

He ran. Janey-Ann was standing, looking back. He stopped when he reached her. He looked back too. "There was a Gate. There must have been."

"There was, Ambion, indeed there was," she said. She spoke no longer as one who knew something he didn't. She took both his hands in hers. "This was the only road for you too."

"I could never have gone back," he said. "When the windows fell off, and I first saw a tree as I had never seen it before, that's what I wished for." He closed his eyes tightly and shook his head. "I wished never to see the city again."

His face felt the moist air, dense with a pale smell of damp leaves. He opened his eyes in the dimness; he walked on the springy leaf litter; he caught a smoky whiff of pine gum; he pressed with his palms a tall trunk's corky bark, dry, wrinkled and ancient. Janey-Ann gave him a sprig of cedar she had squeezed with her fingers. He raised it to his nostrils, and slowly breathed its green pungency. "This is what I have always longed for, and now I am here."

They stood where the old road had been — the road that only they had used as long as men could remember. They flung themselves down on its grass, breath recovered. The sky was a darkening blue, the chicory closed; the trees wore their night clothes of grey. The air was cool and the shadows deep. Sifting down from the tree tops was a sound like the shaking of tiny tambourines: it was the breeze in the Trembling Aspens. The Gate was gone. The Tower once more was a pale dream. Through a chink in the tall twisted Fence of Unwish, they watched the backs of the Golden Men as they walked away.